The
Red Wings of
Christmas

The Red Wings of Christmas

by Wesley Eure

Illustrated by
Ronald G. Paolillo

PELICAN PUBLISHING COMPANY
Gretna 1992

Library of Congress Cataloging-in-Publication Data

Eure, Wesley.
    The red wings of Christmas / Wesley Eure ; illustrated by Ronald G. Paolillo.
       p. cm.
    Summary: When Albert accidentally climbs into Santa's sack, he finds himself drawn into a conflict between good and bad toys that could result in no toys being given out on Christmas Eve.
    ISBN 0-88289-902-3
    [1. Toys—Fiction. 2. Christmas—Fiction. 3. London (England)—Fiction.] I. Paolillo, Ronald G., ill. II. Title.
PZ7.E872Re   1992
[Fic]—dc20   92-5457
                                       CIP
                                       AC

Manufactured in the United States of America

Published by Pelican Publishing Company, Inc.
1101 Monroe Street, Gretna, Louisiana 70053

*To my dear friend John Allison, whose
journey with the Red Wings taught me
much about life . . .*

Contents

Chapter 1   *The Journey*   11
Chapter 2   *The Mud Lark*   17
Chapter 3   *The Toy*   21
Chapter 4   *A Time of Love*   27
Chapter 5   *The Loss*   33
Chapter 6   *The Shelter*   37
Chapter 7   *The Snowflakes*   39
Chapter 8   *The Handyman*   47
Chapter 9   *The Recovery*   55
Chapter 10   *The Ballerina*   57
Chapter 11   *The Understanding*   65
Chapter 12   *The Plan*   71
Chapter 13   *The Battle of the Paintbrushes*   77
Chapter 14   *The Secret*   81
Chapter 15   *The Jacks*   87
Chapter 16   *The Fortress*   93
Chapter 17   *The Queen*   97
Chapter 18   *The Challenge*   103
Chapter 19   *The Sideshow*   107
Chapter 20   *The Flight*   111
Chapter 21   *The Spy*   115
Chapter 22   *The Pond*   123
Chapter 23   *The Trojan Horse*   129

Chapter 24	*A Time to Go*	133
Chapter 25	*The Out-of-Step Dancer*	139
Chapter 26	*The Wayward Glow*	145
Chapter 27	*The Discovery*	149
Chapter 28	*The Reunion*	153
Chapter 29	*The Good-byes*	161
Chapter 30	*The Shawl*	167

The
Red Wings of
Christmas

CHAPTER ONE

The Journey

IT WAS THE KIND OF DAY when legends begin.

A great storm was under way. The mighty waters churned in fury, tossing the Atlantic paddle-wheeler from wave to wave.

Heavily ladened, the *HMS Discovery* had set sail just two days before on the seventeenth of August, 1851, from the Port of London. The treacherous and unpredictable waters of the English Channel smashed against her sturdy timbered hull. She was no match for their intensity.

Sailors scurried frantically among frightened passengers, trying to secure the ship.

High on the mainmast, several brave sailors clung to the tangled rigging urgently trying to release the torn canvas sails.

The towering iron smokestack belched clouds of black carbon as terrified hands stoked coal into her fiery belly. The paddle boxes rattled as the great wheels battled the raging sea.

Lightning and thunder set the darkened sky to glowing and vibrating with a strange and unearthly rhythm. The old-time sailors were humbled by the eerie yet magical quality of this tempest, for this was a storm unlike any storm they had ever seen.

William Trotter and his wife, Sarah, had boarded the ship in London to follow a dream, to start a new life in America. Now fear alone enveloped them.

When William found no refuge in the already overcrowded bowels of the ship, he was forced on deck to search for protection for his wife, who was carrying an oversized bundle.

Then he spotted the ropes tied to the mizzenmast. If he could reach them, maybe they would be safe.

William grabbed Sarah's shoulders as he desperately moved her, holding onto their belongings. They fought through the panic on deck to reach their destination.

At last! The ropes! William struggled to lash his wife to the creaking timber of the mast. Cascades of icy water broke over them, as mammoth waves pounded away at the ship.

Sarah tightened her arms around her precious bundle, a tiny one-year-old child lying in his small wooden cradle. Humming an ancient lullaby, she tried to soothe her crying infant and remember calmer days, the days when William had so painstakingly carved the beautifully ornate cradle in anticipation of the birth of their first and only child. And she remembered how he had so proudly carved the name of their son in the headboard—Albert.

Screams of anguish broke her thoughts. In the commotion around her, she saw a child who had been wrenched loose from her family try desperately to run back to them. The little girl kept losing her footing on the heaving wet deck.

"My granddaughter! For God's mercy! Please . . . someone, grab hold of my granddaughter!" cried an old woman.

At that moment Sarah reached out and grabbed the terrified child, momentarily loosening her hold on Albert's wooden cradle.

Then the unthinkable happened.

A giant hand of a wave reached over the ship's deck and grabbed the cradle from Sarah's grip. It retreated back over the metal safety railing, hurling its small treasure into the great expanse of water.

Sarah's terror-filled screams were lost in the tumultuous claps of thunder. Her baby! She had to get to Albert! She clawed at the ropes binding her, trying to free herself to dive into the ocean after him.

But William's hands held her back as the distance between the ship and the tiny wooden cradle grew ever greater. The sight of the tiny helpless vessel bobbing and rocking on the mighty waters was soon obscured. The billows of smoke from the *Discovery's* chimney disappeared from the horizon, as the ship plowed its way on toward America.

Soon after the cradle was out of sight, the weather began to change. As quickly as the storm had appeared, it was gone. Beams of sunlight broke through the black clouds and smiled down upon the little lost boy; and as the beams grew ever brighter, they began to dry out the soaked blankets covering him.

The elements banded together to care for the child Albert. Subsiding whitecaps began to caress and gently rock the cradle, now acting as a small boat for its lone passenger. The sun warmed Albert as the currents pushed the vessel along its way. A warm gust of wind playfully circled the cradle and steered it in an easternly direction. The elements assumed control of this small sailor's destiny.

For the next day, Albert's new protectors saw to most of his needs; but hunger set in. And the rumbling of his stomach caused him to cry.

A large white sea gull with black-tipped wings soared high above. Escorting her fledgling on his first flight, she heard Albert's cries and noticed the lone craft bobbing far below. Guiding her baby, she glided down and they came to rest on the headboard. Instantly she saw the reason for the cries—an empty bottle. The mother gull instructed her baby to stay with the infant. He started to protest but it was too late. She was gone.

When the baby bird could see her white and black feathers no more, he turned to study the boy. Suddenly the impish warm gust of wind pushed the unsteady little creature into the cradle.

Startled, they stared at each other. Soon the curious Albert ceased his crying and reached out to stroke his new playmate's feathers.

Almost an hour passed before the mother gull's shadow flickered over the cradle. Swooping down, she saw her son and the baby laughing and playing and she smiled. When the baby bird saw his mother, he opened his mouth in anticipation. Immediately she reached over with her beak and deposited some berries she had picked for them. Albert imitated his new friend and opened his mouth. She turned from her own baby and dropped some of the crushed berries into the boy's waiting mouth. Hungrily, Albert swallowed the food.

Three days had passed since the storm had churned up the waters of the English Channel. Much debris floated into the mud flats along the shores of the River Thames.

It was a cold day, colder still along the riverbank. A solitary figure stooped over its waters, oblivious to the chill, patiently washing a large pile of dirty clothes.

Tezzy, an old, fat washerwoman, sang her favorite English tune as she had done so many days of her life, but her joyful melody was interrupted by faint sounds. A baby laughing? Where?

The curious woman looked around. There in the river, floating safely on the incoming tide, was a small wooden cradle. Perched on top of the headboard were the two gulls.

Though she could not swim, Tezzy waded fearlessly through the icy currents of the Thames to see if her suspicions were true. Was there a child lying within?

As she reached out to grab the cradle, the mother bird and her baby squawked and flew into the air, but continued to circle, making sure Albert was in no danger.

Slipping on the muddy bottom, Tezzy fell headfirst into the water. But somehow she managed to hold onto Albert's cradle.

Despite the strong current, the large woman maneuvered her way back onto the riverbank. Drenched and shivering, she gazed into the cradle.

"Well, look at what the sea 'as brought us then . . . a little sailor boy," she laughed as she lifted the smiling child.

Satisfied that the boy was now in good hands, the mother gull nudged her offspring. It was time to leave. Reluctantly, the baby bird turned and flew away from his newfound playmate.

Feeling a chill, Tezzy laid the small boy back into his cradle and quickly gathered the rest of her belongings, tossing them into her basket. She lifted the cradle atop the basket and hurried her way into London.

The small gust of wind that had helped guide Albert here blew, once more, into his cradle as if to say good-bye before it headed out to sea.

Albert had begun his new life.

CHAPTER TWO

The Mud Lark

ALBERT WALKED ALONG the mud flats of the River Thames, as he did each day except Sunday, happily collecting pieces of coal and driftwood or anything else he could find. He put his treasures into the frayed burlap sack he carried, until he could take them to town to sell.

Seven years had passed since he had floated into his new life with Tezzy. Now eight years old, Albert had become one of the throngs of poor children in London who scavenged the banks for anything that could be sold. Albert was a "mud lark," one of the dirty, mud-covered street urchins who went about their business always singing.

Tezzy had taught Albert many songs and he was humming her favorite when suddenly he stopped. "This should fetch me a half-penny!" he exclaimed, spying a large piece of coal. "Tezzy's gonna be proud of me today, she is!"

Picking up the soggy piece of coal, he resumed his song but again he stopped. The singing of an approaching group of boys urged him to put his find hurriedly inside the sack. It was too late.

"There's that little lost boy! Let's see what 'e's got in 'is bag!" cried one of the gang.

Albert knew he had to protect his find. Tezzy needed the money it would bring. Clutching his treasures tightly, Albert began to run. The group of mud larks yelled for him to stop and threw handfuls of gooey mud in his direction.

Albert ran at full speed until he came to a bend in the river where many large pieces of earthen pipe had been abandoned. Ducking into one of the largest pipes, Albert hid himself. Over his rapid breathing, he heard his attackers squishing in the mud.

"Hey! Wait! Where did that little lost boy go?"

"I think 'e's right 'ere somewhere."

Albert held his breath.

"Don't worry! We'll find 'im! And when we do . . ."

"Yeah, looked like 'e 'ad plenty of stuff in 'is sack! Good ole Albert is always good for a big 'aul," smirked Kettle, the leader of the gang. "Keep looking!" Kettle's soot-covered face was as black as an old teapot.

A piece of coal fell from the torn seam of Albert's sack, causing a loud ringing against the hard-glazed pipe.

Albert froze.

"Did you 'ear that?" challenged Kettle.

"Yeah! Think I'm deaf?" snarled Smudge, his second in command.

"'E's got to be in one of those pipes," Kettle announced loudly for Albert to hear. "Come on, lads; I always like a good game of 'ide-'n-seek."

Kettle reached into his sack and pulled out a club of gnarled driftwood. The other boys followed his lead, pulling pieces of wood from their sacks.

Kettle snickered, "Oh, Albert. Don't 'ide from us. We just want to be your . . . friends."

Kettle raised his stick and whacked it against one of the pipes. A dull bonging sounded. The other boys, taking his cue, began bonging on other pipes.

Albert was trapped! The boys were getting nearer. Their jeering and pounding came closer. Each hit was followed with globs of mud tossed into the openings of the pipes.

Suddenly Kettle stopped. He'd noticed footprints in the mud leading to one of the larger pipes. Aha! Could it be? He motioned for the others to stop and pointed to the footprints. They all smiled and nodded knowingly.

Inside the pipe, the silence seemed interminable to Albert. Had they found him?

One of the younger mud larks could not hold his excitement and started to laugh. He was silenced quickly by a hard shove from Kettle.

Albert crouched down farther into his hiding place. Again the silence was broken by a noise—only this time from inside the pipe. Albert blinked into two red eyes staring up at him. His heart was pounding faster. He blinked again. He was looking straight into the red eyes of a large river rat, that vicious creature which every English child knew carried deadly diseases. Albert's mind raced as he remembered the horrible stories of rodents attacking people, especially children. A shiver ran down his spine as he tried to remain perfectly still.

Strangely, a sense of calm and purpose overtook him. He slowly unbuttoned his jacket and removed it. Then with one quick and accurate move, he tossed the coat and captured the rat. Startled, the rat started to fight and claw its way out of the trap. But Albert grabbed the ends of the jacket together and lifted the rodent into the air. From inside the thick material, the rat began to squeal.

"I think I 'ear 'im there," whispered Kettle.

He signaled Smudge and two of the other boys to the opposite end of the long pipe to block Albert's escape. Then he moved toward the opening where the footprints led. He reached down for a handful of mud as the other boys followed suit.

Albert watched the shadows move across the ground in front of his cylinder prison. The rear, he thought. He could escape from the other end! But no. He turned to see shadows moving there, too. He was trapped.

The rat's cries, although muffled by Albert's jacket, could still be heard from outside the pipe.

Several other rats began to emerge from their hiding places to help their captured friend. Slowly, they began to creep toward the pipe.

Kettle gave the sign. The mud larks began yelling, banging on the pipe, and tossing mud into both openings. The noise was deafening. Albert was pinned by the growing walls of mud.

"All right, boys! Go in and get 'im!" commanded Kettle. "We've got you now, you orphan boy!"

Kettle and the others started to enter. But no! Albert couldn't let them catch him! There was only one thing left to do. Albert threw his jacket toward Kettle at the front entrance, freeing the terrified rat from his cloth net.

At that moment the other rats came into view, and baring their teeth, raced toward their now-freed brother. Kettle, in his urgency to get away, tripped over his own feet and fell, skinning his left elbow and barely escaping the snapping rats.

Smudge and the others climbed on top of the large pipes in fear; but almost as quickly as the rats had appeared, they scurried back into their secret hiding places.

The way now clear, Albert crawled through the mud and darted out the front. He picked up his jacket and ran for London Bridge.

The other boys gave chase.

"Don't let 'im get away," yelled Kettle, nursing his sore arm.

They were gaining on him. Albert picked up speed and rounded a bend in the river. Suddenly a huge fallen tree blocked his path!

As he struggled to climb over the obstacle, his foot got caught in a branch. Escape seemed impossible. Desperately, he fought to free himself as the mud larks drew closer. With one hard, painful jerk, his foot broke free from the tree's grip, but the movement sent him tumbling to the ground on the other side. Free! Albert grabbed his burlap sack to run, but it caught on a thorny limb. He pulled and pulled! It tore open, spilling its contents—his whole day's work—to the ground. There was no time to gather his treasures. He raced on.

Sighting the ripped sack and the scattered coal and wood, the mud larks forgot all about Albert. Instead they fought amongst themselves over the spoils, leaving the mud-splattered Albert to run unpursued, but empty-handed, toward home.

CHAPTER THREE

The Toy

LONDON WAS A TEEMING CITY, its streets filled with people and horses. The smoke billowing from the chimneys of factories and homes gave the air a pungent odor and a misty quality. There was much poverty to be seen as its citizens struggled to make a life. But Albert saw none of this as he headed straight for the run-down shack he shared with Tezzy.

Though usually playful and full of life, Albert, depressed about losing his whole day's work, did not dawdle on his way home this day. Tezzy had been ill recently, and he wanted to make sure that this woman, who had been like a mother to him, was cared for. He was very upset to be going home empty-handed when her need was so great now.

Albert walked briskly down the cobblestone streets until he reached the section he called home. People waved at him and called out greetings. Mr. Hutchinson, the old baker, ran out of his shop carrying two crusty ends of bread.

"Albert, me boy," he called out. "Take these to Tezzy. And make sure you tell 'er I hope she'll be up and around real soon. Sure do miss 'er singin'!"

"Uh, thank you, Mr. 'Utchinson. I will." And Albert hurried on his way. He couldn't stop to chat today.

But every little boy had his weakness, and Albert was no exception. His pace slowed as he neared Mr. Lacy's Toy Emporium. This was Albert's oasis from the harsh world in which he was forced to live. It was magical. No matter that the building was decaying and its sign fading, for just inside the massive front door, fantasy became reality.

Albert had to stop. He peered through the magic window as he had done every day for as long as he could remember. The display shelves were packed. Christmas was but a few days off. But this was a poor neighborhood, so the toys inside were not elaborate or expensive. They were mostly common toys, but––oh—the dreams they offered were priceless.

21

❄

The neighbors couldn't remember a time when this shop had not occupied this southwest corner of Wapping High Street and Fisherman's Lane.

The front door of the shop swung open and out stepped the owner, a small white-haired man with a slight limp, requiring the use of a cane—Mr. Lacy, by name.

"Afternoon, boy. I suppose you 'ave come to see your old friend again," he said knowingly, inviting Albert in.

"Oh, no, sir. I really must 'urry 'ome today," he replied and turned to leave.

"Oh, I see then. How is ole Tezzy today?" Mr. Lacy inquired with special concern in his voice.

"She'll be fine. 'Er medicine seems to be making her better every day."

"I s'pect so," Mr. Lacy chuckled. "Tezzy's stronger than the queen's coach team! And no finer lady ever lived in Buckingham Palace than what Tezzy is. Well, come on in then. If she's doing that well, you can spare enough time for me to wind it up for you." He led Albert into the wondrous room.

The musty smell of an ancient attic greeted the boy as he entered.

"Mr. Lacy, I sure am glad you 'aven't sold it yet."

Mr. Lacy got the ladder to make the hard climb to the top shelf.

"Don't suppose I will in this neighborhood," he responded. "The blinkin' thing costs too much." Slowly, awkwardly, he climbed the ladder. "It's been taking up room on me shelves for near five times your age."

He reached for the object of Albert's daily pilgrimage. There on the top-most shelf of the window was a large, beautifully painted, green-jeweled music box.

"Lot's of dust up here," he sneezed. "Better tidy up a bit. Christmas is coming, and I got to make these windows look good if I expect to sell anything."

Mr. Lacy cautiously came down the ladder and placed the music box on the counter in front of Albert.

"Mr. Lacy," Albert asked, "tell me once again the story of 'ow you got Quigley?"

"Quigley is it, then? You've given 'im a name today, 'ave you?" laughed Mr. Lacy.

"When you love something," Albert replied as he reached out to touch the music box, "Tezzy says it must 'ave a name. Then it's special. It belongs."

"I suppose that's so," pondered Mr. Lacy, as he took the music box from the counter to study it more closely.

"This one is special all right," he continued. "But by now I'm thinking you must know this story better than me, boy," he chuckled as he looked into Albert's pleading eyes. "Oh all right, I'll tell you the story just once more!" Both knew that this wouldn't be the last time.

"A very long time ago, this Scottish fellow was passing through town with 'is family when 'is 'orse got spooked. Right out there on Fisherman's Lane, it was."

"Then what 'appened?" interrupted Albert.

"Well, before you knew it, that 'orse was bucking and running crazy toward me shop. It was all I could do to get out of the way meself before that crazy old mare crashed through me front window. Wrecked all me toys up 'ere in front, it did."

Albert gasped.

"There was glass and broken toys and people and bobbies everywhere. The poor old mare was so cut up that they 'ad to put her out of 'er misery," Mr. Lacy reported sadly.

At this point in the story, Albert always winced. The thought of death was something he could not imagine.

"One of the bobbies got a gun and killed the poor beast," continued the old man.

"Oh, no," cried the boy.

"Then the fellow's wife started crying, saying they 'ad no money to pay repairs and without a 'orse 'ad no way to earn any. She begged the police not to 'aul her 'usband away."

"Did they take 'im?" asked Albert, completely enraptured with the story.

"Oh, they were going to, all right. But 'is wife saved him. She went and got this—this box you now call 'Quigley'—from a trunk on their broken cart and brought it to me. She asked if it would cover me damages. Said she'd give it to me if I wouldn't press charges. Seeing it was valuable, I settled."

"But, Mr. Lacy, why is it still 'ere?"

"Well, in order to cover me damages, I had to sell it for a lot of money, but nobody in this neighborhood 'ad that kind of money. So I put it on the shelf and over the years, it became like a permanent fixture in the store. It's been 'ere so long, I guess no one will ever take it, not that I 'aven't had some inquiries, but no one's bought it."

"I wish I could buy it," Albert sighed. "But we 'ardly 'ave enough money for the landlord."

"You are the first person in years to really take such an interest in it, me boy," Mr. Lacy smiled.

He stepped back from the music box and took on a fake mystical air. Then he raised his hand close to the box, and whispered, "Are you ready to begin, lad?"

"Oh, yes. Please," Albert replied and his face filled with the joy of expectation.

Mr. Lacy cranked the little handle on the beautiful box. A haunting yet strangely familiar melody drifted from it. Albert laughed with anticipation.

Faster and faster, Mr. Lacy turned the handle. The music filled the store. Around and around the handle spun. Faster and faster the music seemed to play until suddenly, the top flew open and out popped the happiest, most colorful Jack-in-the-box ever to be seen. Although the toy was meant to startle children, its effect was quite the opposite on this boy; he squealed with delight! Even Mr. Lacy, having seen this a hundred times over the years, had to smile.

"Oh, Quigley! You're a wonder!" Albert exclaimed and danced around clapping his hands together. "Isn't 'e, Mr. Lacy?!"

Mr. Lacy agreed and started to repack the Jack-in-the-box. Suddenly Albert's laughter subsided as he remembered his need to get home.

"Well, I best be off. Thanks, Mr. Lacy," Albert said, running out the front door and back into the real world.

"See you tomorrow! And remember, pick up your feet and don't trip," Mr. Lacy yelled after him. Turning back to the music box, he mused to himself, "I better get these shelves dusted off if *I'm* going to pay me landlord."

CHAPTER FOUR

A Time of Love

TEZZY'S HOME WAS A SHACK on the Isle of Dogs, a small peninsula jutting out into the Thames near Wapping. It was a very small place, more a burrow than a building. Most of its contents had been rescued from the London streets. The sofa and chairs had seen far better days. There was evidence of their being patched more than a couple of times, but patched they were. Despite her lack of means, Tezzy kept a clean, well-run house, more so since the day Albert had floated into her life. In one corner of the small lodging, Albert's wooden cradle occupied a place of honor. A feeling of calm was evident everywhere in this loving space.

This had been a cold winter, and the first snow was predicted for this very night. The temperature outside was just at freezing, and inside the shack wasn't much above it. Tezzy was lying in her bed, bundled in tattered quilts to ward off the cold. She had aged greatly in the last seven years. Her hands and face revealed her hard labors. Yet her spirits and humor seemed to give her more life than what was in truth left.

Laughter filled the room as Tezzy exchanged banter with two old cronies. Daisy, an aging, black vegetable seller, was laughing the hardest. Walter, the old blind man, was trying to be more sensible.

"Woman, will you just relax and not get yourself so worked up? You know what the doc said," he scolded.

"Oh, Walter, you've known me for nigh on to fifty years. Do you think I'm going to change me ways now?" laughed Tezzy, her laughter turning into coughing.

"Walter's right. Maybe you should calm down a little, Tezzy dear," said Daisy with concern. "Your coughing will shake the building down," she chided.

"Now don't you start on me, too, Daze," said Tezzy, recovering a bit.

Daisy turned to Walter and with mock grandeur said, "Luv, we 'ad better take it easy or Lady Muck's liable to cut us out of 'er will. Eh, Walter?"

Daisy started laughing at her own joke, but Tezzy laughed even harder.

"I don't think this is funny," scolded Walter. "There are things we need to talk about."

Tezzy ignored him and turned to Daisy, requesting a bit more of her medicine. Walter scoffed, but Daisy happily obliged. She lifted the medicine bottle from the small table to find its contents, the local homemade gin, were almost gone. She poured the last drop into a tin cup for Tezzy, who drank it straight down.

"What about the nipper?" asked Walter, trying to guide the conversation back to a serious note. "We have to talk about the boy."

Albert, covered with mud and winded from his run home, burst through the door.

"Sorry I'm late," he apologized and planted a kiss on Tezzy's forehead.

"I bet you stopped in to see that Mr. Lacy again, didn't you, boy?" she said feigning disapproval.

"Only for a minute, Tezzy. I swear."

"I'm beginnin' to think that toy means more to you than me."

"You know that ain't so. You are me queen, Tezzy," said Albert as he sat next to her on the bed.

"And you are me little sailor. The captain of me fleet," said Tezzy reaching for his hand.

They smiled, for they had used these nicknames a thousand times before.

Albert bent over to give his Tezzy a great hug, but she pushed him away gently.

"Don't you go getting me all dirty there, young man. You are quite a sight, you are. Looks to me like you brought the whole bloody bank of the river with you today. Now you go wash yourself—scoot!"

"Yes, ma'am," Albert obeyed.

He walked over to a large chipped pitcher and bowl near the door, poured some water into the bowl, and, careful not to splash, began to wash off the mud from his day's adventure.

The three friends resumed their conversation, a bit quieter now so Albert could not hear.

"Tezzy, we should talk!" whispered Walter.

"Oh, leave 'er alone," Daisy snapped as Tezzy began to cough. Daisy turned to Walter, who could not hide the worried expression crossing his face.

"You ought not to be workin' out in the cold. You should be 'ome resting. This weather isn't good for what ails you," chided Walter.

"I'm doing just fine," Tezzy reassured, as she recovered from her coughing spell. "Don't you worry about me none."

"It just don't make sense, luv," said Daisy. "Puttin' all that time in to pay for that silly toy to give to the nipper."

Tezzy pulled the quilts around her more tightly. "It makes sense to me. It's the only thing me dear Bert 'as ever wanted, and 'e'd never ask for it. So I decided to work for Mr. Lacy between me other jobs, doing what I could, when I could."

"Humph," interjected Daisy. "Still don't make no sense."

"Daisy," Tezzy continued, "for almost three years I 'ave been scrubbing 'is stoop and doing other odd jobs. We set up an account, we did. We made ourselves a deal. As long as no one walks in and pays 'im outright for it, 'e promised 'e would 'old it for me. In a few days I will 'ave enough in my account to be able to give me little Bert that music box for Christmas."

"You're a crazy old woman, you are," chastised Walter. "You barely got enough to keep you and the boy fed, and 'ere you are wasting your 'ealth and time working for free to get some fancy toy for the lad. And you squander what little money you do 'ave on your so-called medicine."

"Just call me Lady Fancy Knickers! I 'ave me priorities. And that boy's all I really got in this world. I want to make 'im 'appy. And if it means working for that toy, then I'll do it."

Walter scrounged around in his pockets until he found a few coins, and feeling them to determine what denomination they were, handed them to Tezzy.

"'Ere, you stubborn old woman. Take these tanners and go see a real doctor."

"Please, luv," begged Daisy. "Your medicine ain't doing you no real good."

Tezzy sat up and held Walter's outstretched hand.

"I am going to be fine. Me and the boy don't need no charity from you or anybody else," she said and gently pushed Walter's hand aside. Raising her voice a bit, she continued, "Now you two, it's time you both went 'ome and left me and me little sailor alone."

"All right," Walter sighed. "But you ain't 'eard the last from me."

"The day I 'ear the last from you, old man," Tezzy wheezed, "is the day I lose me 'earing altogether."

The old friends laughed aloud at this.

"Now, be gone with you," Tezzy ordered.

Daisy took Walter's hand and helped her blind friend put on his coat for the cold walk home. Still giggling, the three exchanged good-bye hugs and promises to see each other in the morning.

"You take care of our old girl! We'll see you in the morning, Albert," said Daisy. Before they shut the door Walter reached out and found a table where he deposited the coins Tezzy had refused.

Tezzy called to a freshly scrubbed Albert, "Let me look at me little sailor, so clean."

Albert moved to Tezzy's bed and sat down.

"All right, little sailor, 'ow come you didn't wash away that gloomy face?" Albert avoided her question by reaching into his pocket and pulling out the crusts of bread.

"'Ere, Tezzy. These are from Mr. 'Utchinson. 'E says for you to get better soon," and he placed the bread on the small table next to the bed.

"God bless Mr. 'Utchinson. 'E's a good man," she smiled. "But now, what about you? You look as if you lost your best friend."

Albert told her the story of his day at the riverbank as Tezzy listened compassionately.

"So you see, I didn't 'ave nothin' to bring 'ome to you to sell," Albert concluded tearfully.

Tezzy pulled the boy close, "Listen, me little sailor, what you bring me every time you come home is far more valuable than a few pieces of coal. To be needed is one of life's greatest gifts. To be loved is the greatest gift of all. And all we really ever 'ave in life is the ability to give and receive love. Besides, no matter 'ow bleak today may be, there will always be another tomorrow."

"I love you, Tezzy," Albert sighed.

Tezzy kissed him on the forehead ever so softly, as she resumed, "Seven years ago when I found you floating down the river in that wooden cradle, I thought I 'ad drunk too much of me medicine. But there you were, needin' someone. Needin' me. I 'adn't been needed since me old man left me. And that was too long ago to count. I guess 'e decided 'e didn't like that I only 'ad one tooth."

Tezzy roared with laughter. She liked her own jokes. They had always kept her going. Then she turned to look at Albert's old cradle sitting in the corner of her bedroom.

"You know, when I brought you 'ome, someone 'ad to tell me that your name, 'Albert,' was carved there on the wood since I can't read. We tried to find out whose baby you were and where you came from, but never did. You must wonder sometimes who you are, and I 'ope someday you find out. But if you do find your real mum and dad, know in your 'eart that there ain't no person who could love you any more than me, me little sailor boy. I'll always be with you."

Tezzy's coughing interrupted her. She reached for her bottle of medicine, but the bottle on the small table was empty.

"Bert, luv, do your queen a favor and fetch me some more from Mr. Weston, the barber."

From her apron pocket she produced a farthing and handed it to Albert. "Now don't you stop to pay no visit to Mr. Lacy."

Albert went to the door but the sound of another cough drew him back to stand at her bedside. Gently, he rubbed her forehead.

"You ain't goin' to leave me, are you, Tezzy?" he pleaded.

"No, I'm afraid, me little sailor boy, you are stuck with your old queen. That I promise."

Albert leaned over and kissed her on her now moist forehead.

"Now be off with you! And take me shawl from the chair. Wrap it around you good. It's perishin' cold out there."

Albert was doing as she said when another, harder cough stopped him.

"What are you waiting for, boy? Be off with you!" she bellowed.

Albert opened the door and bolted out, forgetting to close it.

"Bert, ain't you forgetting somethin'?" yelled Tezzy.

He reappeared, realizing he forgot the door.

"Sorry about that."

Tezzy laughed, saying, "I swear you got some water on the brain from your little river voyage. Now scoot."

"I do love you," Albert said.

"Then 'urry up, lad, and get back 'ere quick," she protested. Albert slammed the door, causing the whole room to shake.

Tezzy heard him bound down the stairs and laughed, "And I do love you, me little sailor."

Albert ran down the stoop and heard her laughter turn into coughing. He was determined to make it back in record time.

CHAPTER FIVE

The Loss

THE FIRST SNOW HAD BEGUN. The dark streets, usually littered with debris, were topped with a clean layer of white frosting. Albert ran into the street and the wind stung his face. The sun had set early on this winter's night. The glow of the gas lamps reflected on the snow blanket, causing it to sparkle.

The first snowfall was always a wondrous time. The streets became a playground. Laughter came from all directions. In the alley a mongrel dog snapped at the snowflakes as they tickled his nose.

Albert hurried on to the old barber's shop. It was a tired Mr. Weston who responded to Albert's urgent knocking.

"May I guess Tezzariah needs more medicine, eh, lad?"

"Yes, sir," he said as he handed over the farthing.

Mr. Weston left the door for a few moments and returned with a small bottle, and Albert was quickly on his way. This time he chose a shortcut that would lead him back by Wapping High Street and Fisherman's Lane. If he couldn't stop, at least he could look.

As Albert passed the warmly lighted toy store, he saw Mr. Lacy up on his ladder dusting the shelves. The old man saw him and waved for him to come inside; at that very moment, he momentarily lost his balance. In his struggle to regain his footing, the feather duster he was holding collided with the cherished music box, sending it tumbling to the ground.

Albert watched in horror as his favorite toy crashed on the floor with such force that it tore Quigley from the shattered box.

A terrifying chill raced through Albert's body! He dropped the bottle of gin; and before it, too, crashed to the ground, he started his mad dash home to Tezzy.

He arrived to see strange men placing a body, covered with a white sheet, onto the back of a horse-drawn cart.

33

"No! No! Not me Tezzy!" he ran screaming. "Tezzy! Please don't leave me! You said you wouldn't! You promised!"

Two black hands came out to encircle him and hold him back.

"She's gone, boy. She's gone."

Albert looked up to see Daisy, tears streaming down her face. As the cart pulled away, its wheels clattered over the cobblestones.

"You broke your promise. You said you wouldn't leave," Albert cried in disbelief.

The sounds of yelling and fighting made Albert turn toward his home. Three men came down the stoop carrying his and Tezzy's belongings and tossed them into the snow. The crowd of onlookers rushed for them like vultures, tearing after the same piece of meat.

Albert broke from Daisy's arms and ran toward the building. Before he could enter, a man in a heavy topcoat stopped him.

"And just where do you think you're going, young man?"

"To Tezzy's flat!" Albert protested, attempting to move the man out of his way.

"She doesn't live there anymore, lad."

"But me things!"

"She was behind in her rent. I'm claiming everything up there as my back rent. Not that that'll do me a lot of good. Nothing of value, as I could see."

Albert looked up the stairs to see another man bringing his old wooden cradle out.

"That's mine!" he screamed.

"I'm afraid that's not so," replied the landlord.

"But it's all I 'ave left!" Albert yelled, trying to push the man out of the way. But he wasn't strong enough to move the man. He slipped on the new-fallen snow and fell into the landlord, who in turn fell back against the workman carrying the cradle. The workman dropped the cradle. It bounced down the stoop and began to split apart. As it landed on the pavement, the headboard broke loose.

The crowd, which had momentarily recoiled, now pushed back in. Kettle and Smudge grabbed the cradle and pulled it apart.

"Well, this ought to make good firewood," Kettle sang out and ran off laughing, holding the headboard high.

"That's mine! Give it back," Albert cried.

The mud larks ran in different directions. Albert followed after Kettle but was given the slip when Kettle jumped over a fence and cut through an alley. Albert had lost him, and slowly he turned back home.

The mob had left and all was quiet. The new-fallen snow had quickly covered up any evidence of the gathering of people only a short time before. Had it been a dream? His heart knew the truth.

Suddenly the night air seemed much colder. He wrapped his scarf tightly around him in an effort to bring warmth, and only then remembered he was still bundled up in Tezzy's shawl. Clutching the tattered yarn, he smelled the faint trace of lye soap Tezzy had always used. Its clean freshness flooded his mind with remembrances.

Wearily he turned to walk away. Where? He knew not. He walked and walked.

The snow that continued to fall heavily during his hours of wandering stopped and a large, full moon appeared through the thickly clouded sky. London had been transformed into a crystalline city. It was very late. No other people were on the streets, so the snow lay glistening smooth over everything.

As if a heavy weight had fallen on him, the day's events caught up with him. He was tired, very tired.

For the first time, he became aware of his surroundings. Where was he? How long had he been wandering? He looked around to see the great Tower Bridge silhouetted in the moon's glow.

"I suppose that's as good a place as any to sleep tonight," he mumbled to himself.

Albert hurried along the riverbank toward the ancient structure. Frigid wind whipped off the water's surface, so he ran for protection toward one of the giant supports of the bridge. Tired and drained, he settled himself at the foot of the support, but sleep seemed a long way off.

The wind whistled through the muffled streets. Only the great bell of Bow Church, the legendary heart of Cockney London, rang out above the sound of the wind as it pierced the snow-carpeted city.

"One, two, three . . ." Albert counted each chime until the final—the twelfth—rang out.

"It's midnight," he said aloud softly. "The beginning of a new day. Tezzy was right. There is a tomorrow."

Albert wasn't aware of the heavy fog rolling in, nor of the faint sounds of sleigh bells muted by the lonesome moans of foghorns on the barges struggling up the Thames.

There was no reason for Albert to look up at the moon slowly being hidden by the fog. But if he had . . . he would have seen the faint silhouette of a sleigh being pulled by reindeer across its glowing white surface. Would he have been able to see the old man holding the reins? No one will ever know. But what is known is that those few brief moments would change his life forever.

CHAPTER SIX

The Shelter

ON THE NIGHT OF THE FULL moon before December twenty-fourth, Father Christmas hitches the reindeer to his sleigh and takes them on a practice run. After a year of idleness, it is necessary that all run smoothly. There can be no mistakes on Christmas Eve if he is to deliver every present before sunrise.

Like the countless times before, the snow-haired gent neared the end of his trial run. Everything was working fine, so he turned his team northward and headed home. Then it happened.

That impertinent warm gust of wind reappeared and blew into Father Christmas's sleigh, lifting his great red toy sack into the air. When it came down, the sleigh had flown on. The sack tumbled and twirled gently down to earth. Like an impish child, the warm gust came back to play with it, sometimes filling it with air like a parachute, sometimes twirling it around like a matador's cape, only to be lifted up again by the stronger cold air currents.

Far below, Albert sensed the fog closing in around him, making him feel very small and isolated. He could see no more than a few feet in front of him.

Then his world went black! Something had fallen on him!

Startled, he screamed, "Don't 'urt me!" Thinking he was being attacked by thieves, Albert cried, "I ain't got nothin' to give you!"

But no one spoke. Silence!

"Anybody out there?" he yelled.

Still no reply. Cautiously he crawled out from under the enormous object. Peering about, he saw nothing.

"'Ello?" he yelled. Again silence. Satisfied he was alone, he felt safe to turn his attention to the mysterious canopy that had fallen on him.

"Well, what do we 'ave 'ere?" he asked in astonishment as he examined the fine quality of its material.

Rubbing his hands across lush white fur, he sighed, "This is fit for a king! I bet I can sell you for a lot of money tomorrow, I can."

Excited, he started to gather up the great expanse of fabric.

"Now what are you and where did you come from?" he questioned, stopping to look around.

Remembering where he was, he nervously glanced up. "I bet some fine gentleman must 'ave dropped this as 'e passed over the bridge. You must be 'is cape or something. 'E's sure to be looking for you! Time for us to find a new place to sleep!"

Albert tried to gather the rest of the material, anxious to flee this spot. But he had some difficulty because of the heaviness of the cloth. At last he managed to get it all in his arms, and started down the riverbank.

The fog had lifted a bit now, but it still gave him enough cover to search for a new hiding place. Where should he go? Then he remembered—the stone statue of Queen Victoria in the park!

Albert raced toward his destination. The temperature in London continued to drop and even Tezzy's shawl couldn't protect him any longer. He smiled when he reached the park. Tonight this statue, this stone lady, would be his "queen."

Crawling up into one of the large carved folds of the queen's dress and pulling the furry expanse of his new "find" around him, he settled into a snug and drowsy state.

He began to feel warm and protected for the first time in hours.

"Tomorrow I can get some money for you. But tonight you will give me some warmth. Tezzy'd be proud of me. I bet I could get enough money to keep 'er in medicine for a long time."

Then he remembered his loss and the pain crept back. Shuddering, he pulled the material snugly around him. It seemed to comfort him, radiating love. What a surprise! What was this that could bring him so much peace?

The fog continued to lift and the moon reappeared from behind the clouds, casting an iridescent glow by which Albert could get a better look at this strange material. The white fur formed a big circle—around an opening! An opening? Sure, that was it! An opening to a bag! A large bag!! Maybe there was something inside that could bring him more money! He poked his head in, but saw nothing. Emptiness. Then a burst of warm air came blowing out. No! Albert's imagination was working overtime. He was so tired, his mind must be playing tricks. He needed sleep. Finally the warmth and comfort made his eyes grow very heavy. At last he could take refuge in sleep. If the sack was empty, he could crawl inside. It would be even warmer there. The sack could be both a tent and a blanket for him.

Finding the opening again, he spread the fur trim apart. To his astonishment a great rush of warmth poured out again. He crawled inside.

"Ahhhh," he screamed. Albert was falling! And falling! And falling!

CHAPTER SEVEN

The Snowflakes

"'ELP ME! WHAT'S 'APPENING? Tezzy! 'ELP ME!"

Faster and faster, Albert's little body tumbled through the black void. Over and over he twirled. Dizzied, he reached out hoping to grab hold of something, but found nothing. Down and down his rapid descent continued.

"'Ellllp!"

But the only response was his own voice echoing. Deeper and deeper through the darkness he fell.

Clunk! He finally landed on something! But now—he was sliding. Whoosh! Down a chute—an invisible chute that twisted and curved.

Then Albert saw a small circle of light. Faster and faster he slid toward it.

Zip! A dazzling beam of red light spun past Albert.

"What was that?" he screamed, his fear increasing.

Down and down. A beam of green light shot up from the faraway circle.

Whiz! Whiz! More shafts of light zoomed past, filling the blackness.

The bright lights blinded Albert as he continued to twist and turn down the slide.

"'Elp! Somebody, please 'elp me! Where am I?" Albert hadn't noticed that the slide had stopped as he hurled through the void now filled with many rays of colored light.

Without the slide to guide him, Albert was falling free, faster and faster, tumbling and twisting, toward the ever-increasing circle of light.

"Oh, noooo!" he screamed when he saw he was about to crash into it.

He closed his eyes tightly to brace himself. But instead of crashing, he heard only the soft tinkling of bells. He hadn't crashed! And he was floating, not falling!

Albert opened his eyes. More colored light filled the space, giving definition to it. It was a cylinder. He was floating through a large cylinder!

"This has got to be a dream!" reason told him. He kept drifting down, farther and farther. But where? Toward what? Albert looked down and, to his astonishment, saw a large snowflake—of light. It reminded him of something. What?

Mr. Lacy's toys! That was it!

"I'm falling through a kaleidoscope!"

He watched as the large snowflake changed shapes and intermixed colors. How beautiful!! The shapes and colors blinked in continual motion as he drifted gently down toward the center of their ever-changing patterns. Lost in their majesty, his thoughts returned to Tezzy. The mixture of the bell sounds around him and the rainbow-colored patterns below transported him back to St. Paul's Cathedral last Christmas Eve. Tezzy was holding his hand, showing him the great stained-glass windows, and telling him the stories. . . .

"Oh, nooo! Not again!" Suddenly Albert's speed increased once more. He was falling toward the very center of the great snowflake. It grew larger and larger. Faster and faster he tumbled, down and down. The tinkling of the bells grew louder and louder until it was deafening. Brighter and brighter the lights became, blinding him.

"'Elp me! Please! Somebody!" he screamed, frightened.

His cries were smothered by the loud clanging of the bells.

He tried to open his eyes, but all he could see were lights surrounding a black circle. This time he was sure he was going to crash and again closed his eyes.

His body tumbled over and over toward the center of the great snowflake. He reached the black circle, but instead of crashing, he silently slipped through, straight down until, despite his rapid speed, softly and gently he landed on something firm. What now?

Cautiously Albert opened his eyes just as someone or something grabbed him. Then there were other hands—or other things—on him, picking him up and carrying him. What was happening?

"Let's get him out of here!" a voice shouted.

"I hear them coming!" from another.

"Hurry, hurry," echoed many voices.

"To The Forest! To The Forest! Quickly, quickly," panicked voices urged each other as they ran off with him.

"Oh, no! Here come the Grablies!" he heard one of them yell as the hands which had been holding him let go.

Standing on his own, Albert was finally able to look around. What he saw wasn't real. It couldn't be.

Again he was lifted. This time by a bejeweled elephant who swooped him up in his trunk and galloped full speed ahead.

He had to be dreaming!

Suddenly a strange thundering sound roared up behind them, sounding like a great army marching slightly out of step.

"Faster, Horseradish!" cried a panda to a . . . a . . . red rocking horse?

"We're almost there! The Forest will be safe," answered the crimson horse.

Screams and shouts came from the direction of the marching sounds.

"Begging your pardon, I am unable to carry you any farther," said the breathless elephant to Albert. "Is it possible for you to run yourself unassisted?"

"What? Are you talking to me?"

"Of course we are," demanded Horseradish. "Are you working?"

"What?" stammered Albert, not understanding any of this.

"Whatever you use to make yourself move! Is it functioning?" demanded the panda.

"Well, I think so," replied Albert and he was released from the elephant's trunk and placed back on the ground. "But what's going on here?"

> "Run, don't talk!
> "Race, don't walk!"

scolded a large top as it spun by.

The thunderous sounds and shouts grew closer. Albert looked in every direction, not knowing what to do. The loud toot of an off-key trumpet blared from the middle of the clamor.

"'Ey! Wait for me!" Albert screamed and ran to catch up with the others, deciding it was better to follow them than get trapped in the fury behind him.

"Please, if you would do me the exquisite favor to hurry up," called Chutney, the ornate Indian elephant, over his shoulder.

Just as Albert caught up, they entered a great maze of cogs, wheels, knobs, nuts, springs, eyes, arms, and many other parts.

> "To The Forest we have made it,
> "For that I'm rather elated,"

cheered the top and briefly stopped spinning.

"Indeed to goodness, everybody hide," trumpeted Chutney.

"What's going on?" Albert demanded.

The thundering sound was much nearer now.

"What word did you not understand? HIDE!!" Horseradish shouted.

The panda reached out and pulled Albert down behind a broken locomotive chassis.

"What's going on?" he insisted again.

> "Silence, or you'll get us all broken,
> "There's danger near and that's no jokin',"

demanded the top.

The source of the noise, a large group of marching toys, came into a clearing near where Albert and the others were hiding. At least they *looked* like they were once toys. Some were missing arms, legs, wheels, and various other parts. And with parts missing, they certainly weren't marching in unison. A very dented and not very shiny trumpet led the way and continued to blare off-key.

"Halt!" commanded a tin soldier with a broken arm.

The army tried to obey, but because of its condition it wasn't easy. Some particularly unstable toys collided into those directly in front of them. Some came to a stop and promptly fell in a heap.

Albert could not help laughing at the sight, but was hushed by the rocking horse. The trumpet blew a shrill and sour note, prompting the tin soldier to turn.

"Will you stop that horrible sound, Fanfare?! I can't hear myself scream!" shouted the rusty soldier.

Fanfare, humiliated by the order, ceased the music.

"Well, they obviously made it to The Forest," continued the tin soldier. "We have no choice but to split up." He began to divide them into three groups.

"Okay, you piles of junk! Bring back new recruits or you'll have to answer to No Name!" he threatened, raising a rusty sword with his one good arm.

The soldier reminded Albert of one of the guards at Buckingham Palace with his large bearskin hat. In his back was a rusty windup key that kept turning.

The three groups stirred with a rumbling of fear.

Then turning his attention to The Forest, the soldier shouted, "All right, you pretty ones! I know you can hear me. You can't hide from us forever! And after we get you, you won't be smiling so pretty. Now, toys! Spread out. All three divisions."

"Yes, sir, Rattles," responded the army, though not in unison.

❄

And off they went—falling over each other, lurching in every direction. Frustrated, Rattles watched this fiasco. He gathered them back together and ordered them out of the clearing. Fanfare's off-key trumpeting was heard fading deeper into The Forest.

Albert started to laugh at this funny sight, but was quickly silenced by the elephant, who covered the boy's mouth with his large trunk.

After a few moments, Albert and the others began to emerge from their hiding places.

"All clear!" shouted Horseradish.

"Now will someone please tell me what's going on?" pleaded Albert.

Before anyone could answer him, a black woman wearing a long red print dress and a bibbed white apron ran up to the group.

"We've got to see Handyman!" she exclaimed.

"Not me! I'm tired, and I'm not going anywhere!" came a honey-voiced Southern drawl from under her skirt.

"Oh, yes you are," insisted the black woman. "Where I go, you go, honey."

"Flop!"

To Albert's surprise, the black woman flipped over and revealed a peaches-and-cream, blonde Southern belle wearing a lacy yellow party dress.

"Deliah, I just can't make it any farther!" sighed Arabella, fluffing out her blonde curls, smoothing her dress. Then noticing Albert, she coyly added, "Well, who have we heah?"

"Flip!" Arabella went to the bottom and Deliah came to the top!

"Arabella, don't you start that again. We have a problem here and we have to solve it," reminded Deliah.

"Well, I'm not going!" retorted Arabella.

"Will you two keep it down? They'll hear us," whispered Horseradish.

But Arabella continued, "If I don't go, you don't go."

"Will you go if I let you go right-side up?" asked Deliah.

"Well . . . all right!" smiled Arabella from under the skirt. "It always works," she whispered to Albert. Then giving the boy a coquettish look, she inquired, "Will *he* be going, too?"

"Oh, not again," sighed Deliah. But after a wink from Horseradish, she said, "Yes. *He's* going, too."

"Flop!"

Arabella, now in the upright position, rearranged herself. Satisfied, she put an arm through Albert's and cooed, "Let's be off, shall we? Now, young suh, you were about to tell me who you are."

"I'm Albert," the frightened boy responded, "but what are you?"

"I'm not a 'what,' suh. I am Arabella," she said with a curtsy.

From under her yellow party dress, Deliah screamed. "Ouch! Will you please let me know before you do that again?"

"Sorry, Deliah," Arabella apologized. Turning back to Albert she continued, "Well, as I was saying before I was so rudely interrupted, Deliah and I are a flip-flop doll from the Magnolia State of Mississippi in America."

"A flip-flop doll?" questioned Albert.

"Yes. Sometimes we are just called Flip-Flop, because when Deliah says 'flip,' we turn so that she is right-side up. And when I say 'flop,' I get to be on top," Arabella explained.

Albert glanced around and realized that indeed these were all large talking toys. Their accents and the other sounds they made were unfamiliar to this untraveled boy for they came from every corner of the globe.

"This is amazing," replied Albert.

Arabella leaned over to him and whispered, "What's really amazing is if she lets me be on top for very long. You see," she confided, "being upside down just ruins my nails, not to mention my hairstyle."

Arabella held out her hands to show the boy the damage to her fingernails caused by having to walk on her hands.

Impatient, the dapper English top, wearing a painted-on tuxedo with striped pants and a monocle over one eye, demanded,

> "Now we don't have time for a delay.
> "Let us to Handyman straight away."

"Right, Topp C. Why don't you twirl ahead and clear the path?" replied Horseradish.

The metallic top spun on and Albert could see his top hat, attached to his windup mechanism, bob up and down, up and down.

The group headed deeper into The Forest. Albert, with Arabella hanging on his arm, was in the middle, walking in a state of shock.

"Wait! Please! Where am I? What is this place?" he pleaded.

"The Forest of Broken Parts, of course," answered Arabella. "You should know that, silly. But I guess maybe you've been away for centuries. Why, of course! That's why you've never had the pleasure of meeting me before."

Albert stared at her, thoroughly confused, figuring it would be better to say nothing. He was sure he would be waking up from this dream soon—wouldn't he?

CHAPTER EIGHT

The Handyman

ALBERT BEGAN TO TAKE note of his surroundings. What an incredible place. Broken parts? Yes, but for what? He walked on and his confusion and fear dissolved to wonderment. A comfortable, easy feeling encompassed him.

Topp C. Turvey spun ahead, keeping a careful lookout for any wayward band of soldiers. His comrades followed, winding their way through the cluttered Forest, taking care to keep very quiet.

First, Albert heard a banging sound, followed by what sounded like a saw cutting wood. The sound of other machines increased as the group walked on.

There in a glade was a knoll. On the small hill was a most marvelous factory. It was a beehive of activity with all sorts of machinery running. Giant wheels turned; pistons hissed up and down. Toys scrambled all over the factory performing their various tasks.

"Well, we made it," sighed the panda.

"And about time. A Southern lady doesn't walk that far; she is usually offered a ride," chided Arabella as she turned to glare at Horseradish.

Deliah poked her head out from under the yellow skirt and exclaimed, "You're tired? I was the one upside down all the way! But now we're home. It's my time, Arabella."

"Oh, not just yet, Deliah," she pleaded and turned her attention back to Albert.

"No arguments!" demanded Deliah.

"Oh, sawdust!" snapped Arabella.

"Flip!"

"Now that's better," said Deliah, right-side up.

A rag doll ran over to the red rocking horse. "I'm so glad you are safe!" she exclaimed.

"Thank you, Fräulein, because we almost didn't make it. My name is Horseradish. Have we met?"

"Oh, silly, you know me. I'm Molly," she giggled.

Horseradish stared hard, trying to remember where they could have met.

Molly laughed again. "You knew me as Molly the sailboat; but while you were away, I went to The Pond and changed. For over one hundred years little boys would play with me in bathtubs and frog ponds and I always ended up being sunk. So I decided to become a girl's toy and play it safe. Now I enjoy a new life, a life of tea parties."

"Ah, Molly," whinnied Horseradish as he finally recognized his old friend. "You look adorable. Some lucky little girl is going to be proud to have you in her life."

Molly giggled, "Oh, I hope so."

Albert, quietly taking all this in, finally said, "What is all this about?"

"Oh, we almost forgot about you," said Horseradish. "Well, we better get you fixed right away."

"Fixed? What do you mean fixed? There ain't nothin' wrong with me," Albert protested.

"But of course there is, or you certainly wouldn't be here," Deliah laughed, taking Albert's hand. "You can trust ole Deliah. Follow me."

"Let me go! Are you all crazy?" screamed Albert as he jerked back his hand.

Then Chutney reached over with his embroidered trunk, scooped him up, and carried him toward the great machinery.

"There's work to be done,
"We've no time to spare.
"Now stop with the fun.
"Let's put you in there,"

Topp C. said, pointing to a strange contraption.

"Goodness to gracious. Yes! Especially in view of the imminent predicament," snorted Chutney.

Albert struggled free from the elephant's trunk. "Don't you touch me! Don't any of you touch me!" he cried. "I may be dreamin', but I ain't goin' to be dragged around!"

Everyone stopped to listen as the argument continued. Even the machinery halted. All attention focused on the loud voices.

Suddenly a warm gust of wind blew through the workshop and with it a hoarse voice called out, slicing through the volume of the argument. "What's the meaning of this?"

Handyman stood in the doorway of a shed near the machines, his ten arms flailing the air. The tools he carried in each of his hands scared Albert.

✳

What was he planning to do with them all? He carried a screwdriver, a wrench, a drill, and other strange tools that were unfamiliar to the boy.

And his appearance! A great tangle of blue hair covered his head and most of his face until it trailed on the floor. His massive body was clothed in a button-down coat with dozens of pockets!

"We have lots of work to do—and no time to do it! Why have you all stopped?" he reprimanded.

"This toy won't get repaired, don't you know?
"He acts as if he's scared, and won't go,"

volunteered Topp C.

"Toy? I ain't no toy! I'm a boy!"

All the toys laughed and jeered at Albert. Horseradish rocked back and forth and whinnied with glee. Topp C. spun rapidly, his hat bobbing up and down, while Deliah and Arabella flip-flopped in laughter. They all began to sputter and clang at this funny new toy's claim. The toys would have seen that even the great Handyman couldn't help smiling, had it not been for his whiskers covering his mouth.

"A boy, is it? I'm afraid that isn't possible. You are a toy," corrected Handyman.

"I ain't a toy!" Albert declared vehemently. "I tell you, I am a boy!"

"Oh, my—my word—
"This *is* absurd,"

chuckled Topp C. as the jubilation continued.

"Boys don't come to Kriss Kringle's sack," explained Handyman.

"Kriss Kringle's sack?" questioned Albert. "Who is Kriss Kringle?"

"Of course you know who he is. Now don't be silly," Handyman firmly stated.

"If all of you toys will just hear me out,
"I'll be glad to tell you what this is about,"

Topp C. interjected,

"That this supposed boy,
"Was tossed from a child's bed,
"And now we find this toy,
"Has crashed and broke his head."

"Yeah, can you fix his head, Handyman?" grizzled the panda.

All the toys became hysterical, breaking into a funny dance around Albert. Chutney stomped up and down causing his jeweled body, stitched with tiny mirrors, to shimmer. Again, the sounds of clanging, snapping, whizzing, and clicking filled the whole workshop.

"Flop!

"Leave him alone! It's not nice to make fun!" yelled Arabella.

"She's right," declared Handyman as he turned to Albert, "but you are a toy, and I want no disagreements."

"But . . ." Albert tried to speak.

"No disagreements. Now, tell me first, what is your name?"

"Albert, sir," he replied.

"All right, Albert. The next step is to clean you up." He reached over, removed Tezzy's old shawl from Albert's shoulders, and nudged him forward, saying, "Now, put him in the Suds Squisher."

"No! Give that back! It's Tezzy's. You can't take that. It's all I 'ave of 'ers!" Albert screamed, jumping for the arm holding the shawl.

"No arguments!" Handyman declared, quickly passing the shawl from one hand to another out of the boy's reach.

The Victorian toys converged on Albert and easily overtook him despite his protests. Samson, a toy boxer made of iron and wearing a white striped undershirt and black britches, lifted Albert up effortlessly.

"Now, take it easy, little toy," the boxer said with a smile which caused his handlebar moustache to lift up.

A few of the other toys came over to assist him with the struggling Albert. They wrestled his body to a table where they removed the remainder of his clothes.

"'Ey, wait a minute!" the embarrassed boy shouted.

Ignoring his pleas, they carried him to a large machine with brushes inside it. Horseradish and the panda began to turn a large crank that started the brushes spinning. Once Albert was inside, three others began to jump up and down on a large balloonlike device filled with soapy water attached to a network of tubing. The sudsy liquids forced through the tubes shot out as a spray from all directions.

"Please, stop this!" he pleaded.

Chutney and Samson ran on a small treadmill that operated the sponge rollers. The rollers sloshed all around his body, mopping up the mud and dirt. Then two mechanical arms lifted him into the air and set him down in a large vat of clear warm water.

"Let me out! Let me out!" cried Albert.

The steam-operated machine ignored his pleas and continued dipping him into the water, up and down, up and down. At last, the arms gently lifted him from the vat and put him on another table.

Just as Albert was about to bolt, four balls took turns bouncing onto a large bellows placed in front of a fire. The warm air that was pushed out began to dry him, while the force of the blowing held him in place.

"Stop this thing!" he demanded.

Despite his protest, there was nothing he could do, and to his surprise, he found that the warmth from the enormous bellows was comforting.

"All right," commanded Handyman. "Dress him."

Two pink rabbits held him until other toys appeared with bolts of colorful material. Panda and Topp C. produced large needles and spools of thread. A baby doll was cutting patterns, while Topp C. began sewing them.

"Ouch!" Albert yelled when Topp C. accidentally stuck him with a needle.

> "Sorry about that, ole chap,
> "For prodding you like that,"

Topp C. apologized,

> "But don't move a lick.
> "This needle will prick."

Albert squeezed his finger, releasing a small drop of blood. An upside-down Arabella was the only one to notice and whispered to Horseradish, "Look, his paint comes from the inside!"

Albert was the center of all activity, until finally the toys were finished.

"Good work. Now let me see. Everyone stand back," ordered the Handyman, clapping his ten hands together.

There stood Albert decked out in a new pair of bright blue britches, glaring red shirt with large black buttons, and an oversized yellow polka-dot bow tie. A pair of black patent leather shoes with turned-up toes provided the finishing touch.

"Oops! Forgot something," said Molly, as she hurried over with a brush and a pail of paint to dab big red circles on his cheeks.

She stepped back, then called for Reflections, the looking glass, who immediately came running over.

Molly said proudly, "Not bad, if I do say so myself."

Albert glared at himself in the mirror and declared, "This looks silly! I want me old clothes back. Give me back me clothes!"

Angrily, he started to wipe off the red circles on his cheeks, which scared the looking glass. It ran to hide behind Molly's dress.

"You look fine, Albert. The toys have done well," Handyman proclaimed. "Now tell me, what do you do?"

"I don't do much of nothin'," protested Albert. "Mostly people tell me what to do."

"That's it then!" Handyman beamed. "You're a puppet!"

The problem was solved! The toys cheered in relief.

"All right, everyone. Get back to work," Handyman ordered. "Time's running out."

Elated, the toys grabbed Albert again, tying strings to his hands and feet in order to make a marionette of him. But he'd had enough! He screamed and broke the strings.

"I ain't no toy! I'm a boy!" he shouted angrily.

The toys withdrew. Albert's behavior frightened them. This emotion—anger—was not known in Kriss Kringle's sack, except by the Broken Army.

"Maybe he's a spy," yelped Horseradish.

At this suggestion, the toys huddled back even farther, fearing he might be a Grablie.

"I'm not a spy! I'm just a boy!"

"Now then, there is no need for that kind of behavior here," Handyman scolded. "You have certainly picked up some regrettable habits during your time out of the sack. You must have belonged to a very unhappy child."

"I don't belong to no one. Why won't you listen?" demanded the boy, removing the broken strings that had been tied to him.

"Well, if you *are* a boy, then how did you get here?" Handyman asked.

Relief crossed Albert's face. Maybe now they would listen. He looked at the toys who had withdrawn but were now creeping back toward him, waiting. All was still as Albert began his story. They hung on his every word.

CHAPTER NINE

The Recovery

A PLUMP OLD MAN in a red suit stepped up to the Queen Victoria statue where the sack lay across her base.

"There you are, my old friend," he said in a deep voice. "I certainly am glad I found you. We would have been in real trouble this Christmas. Now, time we went home." And with that he reached down and picked up the sack. . . .

"What's happening now?" Albert asked as he grabbed hold of Deliah for support, forgetting his story.

The whole Forest, including the workshop, swung wildly back and forth.

"Someone has picked up the sack;
"Now we're riding on his back!"

Topp C. exclaimed.

"A human?" guessed Arabella from under Deliah's skirt.

"Let's just hope it's Kriss Kringle," said Handyman.

All the toys fell silent and listened nervously. What seemed like hours passed until the faint ringing of jingle bells filled the sack. Relieved, the toys let out a cheer.

"It's Kriss Kringle, all right," announced Handyman happily.

"Then everything's okay?" came Arabella's weak voice still under the skirts.

"Not quite, little lady," Handyman pondered. "If Kriss Kringle only knew how bad things were in here, he would really be worried."

This was more than Albert could fathom.

"I don't know what's going on here, but I'm gettin' out!" he yelled and ran full speed toward The Forest, only to be tripped up by his pointed shoes.

"We'll get him!" shouted Horseradish and Samson as they started after him.

"Not necessary. He'll be back," intoned Handyman as he watched the confused boy disappear into The Forest. "Besides, we have too much work to do."

Waving his ten arms he exclaimed, "Now everyone back to work. We have so little time."

The congregation of toys quickly returned to their assigned tasks and once again their machines huffed and puffed and clanged and clattered. Handyman stood quietly and gazed into The Forest.

CHAPTER TEN

The Ballerina

CONFUSED AND SCARED, Albert ran as fast as he could. Maybe he could find a way out of here. Just maybe. But he stumbled.

"I can't run with these on," he mumbled and stopped to pull off the pointed black patent leather shoes.

Angrily, he threw the shoes at some of the broken parts that made up The Forest.

"Now stop that," cried a broken cartwheel as a shoe hit. This Forest was truly alive. Albert panicked and, afraid of being followed, climbed to his feet and ran at full speed.

The once friendly Forest now took on a sinister quality. At every turn, Albert was frightened by broken toy parts that came to life. He couldn't stop running and what was worse, he had no idea where he *was* running. He kept looking over his shoulder to see if he were being followed. He pinched himself hoping he would wake up. But even now he did not really believe that he was sleeping.

He heard something and stopped. He started toward the sound, slowly, carefully. As he got closer, he became aware of beautiful and haunting music filling The Forest. It was a familiar sound, but he couldn't quite place it. The music became clearer as he grew nearer. His heart ached. The melody flooded his mind. It's Quigley's music! An overwhelming feeling of both sadness and joy overtook him.

Albert ventured closer toward the sound. Suddenly a large spring came bouncing by, forcing Albert to avoid a collision by diving into a pile of old material.

The spring yelled as it passed, "Watch, watch, watch, where, where, where, you, you, you, are, are, are, going, going, going."

"Uh, sorry," Albert replied as he stood up to dust himself off.

"Well, well, well, I'm, I'm, I'm, off, off, off," assured the spring and bounced away.

The sound of its boing-boing-boing faded into the heart of The Forest, again to be replaced by the haunting melody of the music.

"This place is loony!" thought Albert.

But the melody—like an old friend—was calling. He walked again toward the music, but this time more cautiously.

He finally reached a small valley, a dingle, with a clearing. Through the maze of parts, he hoped to find Quigley. But to his disappointment, he saw the opened, mirrored lid of a different music box. In the center of the red-jeweled box was poised the most exquisite porcelain ballerina. She moved so gracefully, turning and turning to the melody. He was mesmerized.

"That certainly ain't Quigley's music box," Albert muttered to himself.

The ballerina extended first one and then the other of her elegant, long legs in rhythm to the music. Hypnotically, Albert was drawn toward her. Closer and closer he edged until she noticed him—and quickly stopped.

"Oh! *Bonjour*, monsieur! You startled me," she said in a soft French accent.

Albert was spellbound and could not speak. He had never seen such perfection.

"You like my dance, *oui*?" asked the ballerina.

Albert could only nod "yes."

The ballerina was well aware of the effect she had on her many admirers and motioned for the boy to come closer. Albert obeyed.

"What is your name? My name is Colette," she offered as she curtsied long and low.

Overwhelmed, the boy remained silent.

"Are you not fixed for speech?" she inquired.

Albert looked at her quizzically.

Concerned, the ballerina said, "Perhaps your lip spring, it is broken, *oui*?"

Albert opened his mouth as if to speak, but the words stayed in his heart.

"Monsieur, can you speak?" demanded the impatient Colette.

Suddenly the boy found his voice and blurted out, "You are beautiful!"

Colette was taken back by the sudden outburst, but soon recovered and laughed, "I see Handyman has fixed you, you silly toy."

Albert protested, "I ain't no toy, I'm a . . . ."

But Colette cut him off and sighed, "*Mon dieu*, could it be zat you and I are the same, monsieur? I am not a toy either."

Albert was astonished. At last he had found another human!! But his hopes were dashed when Colette went on to explain.

"I am *un objet d'art*! A museum piece, not a common toy. I do not belong here," she sighed. Albert knew the feeling. "I was one of a pair—my brother and I were created for a prince and a princess. Then ze humans fought a war and we were hidden underground for many years to keep us safe. Years later we were put on display in a museum for all to see. Zen my brother was stolen and for ze last several hundred years I was left alone and never wound up. People came from all over ze world to stare at me, to gaze at my flawless beauty."

"What 'appened?" Albert implored. "Why are you here?"

"*Un enfant terrible!* A nasty little girl slipped by ze guards and wound me up so tightly, she broke my spring." Her lightly accented voice filled with despair. "Zen when Mimi was caught, she drop me and ran crying to her mama! Crash I went. And zen zere were ze Red Wings!" Remembering caused the ballerina to tremble.

"Red Wings?" Albert thought. "What Red Wings?" Things were getting stranger and stranger. "Did this 'Andyman fix you?" Albert asked.

She executed a complete turn to show Albert how perfectly repaired she was. "*Oui*, monsieur. *Le* Handyman is an artist, don't you think?"

Albert told Colette he had to agree and in gratitude she bent down and kissed the boy on the forehead. The embarrassed boy blushed. Albert was in love!

But when a frown crossed his face, Colette asked, "Why so sad, monsieur?"

Albert explained that when he heard her music box play he had hoped he might find Quigley. "You 'ave the same music as a Jack-in-the-box I once fancied," revealed the boy.

Colette was astounded. "*Impossible*! Ze same music? My song is a long forgotten lullaby."

But Albert wasn't listening. His eyes were on the music box. It didn't have the same patterns or the emerald-green jewels, but it looked so much like Quigley's. He reached out to touch one of the precious stones as he had so often done to Quigley's box at Mr. Lacy's Toy Emporium.

"Oh, no, monsieur! Please do not touch zat! I do not want my beautiful home broken again!" Colette pleaded.

Albert quickly pulled his hand back and said, "Sorry. It's just that it looks so much like my old friend's."

"Zis is one of a kind. Zere is no other," she offered. "Now tell me, what are you doing in zis part of the sack? Why aren't you with ze other more common toys?"

"I don't know where I am," sighed Albert.

"Why, monsieur, you are in Kriss Kringle's sack!"

"Please don't laugh . . . but . . . what is this sack?" asked Albert pleadingly. "And who is this Kriss Kringle?"

"But all toys know Kriss Kringle and his great red sack," she insisted.

Albert sighed, "But I don't. Please 'elp me!"

"But, of course, monsieur," she said. "Then zis must be your first time here," she responded more softly. "*Oui*? Is zat not true?"

"Why, yes," Albert replied, "I 'ave never been here before."

"Neither have I," she confessed sadly, "and never imagined such a thing." She seemed to drift away into herself.

Albert broke the silence with, "Won't you please tell me more about this place?"

"It's ze place where all abandoned and broken toys come so they can be fixed up and painted, good as new. Toys are not made here, zey are only repaired. Zat's why children never see broken toys lying around ze house for very long. Zey just . . . disappear," she explained and resumed extending her legs, a bit bored now with all the questions.

There were so many more things he wanted to know. He, of course, had crawled in, but . . .

"'Ow did the toys get here?" he asked.

"I'm not sure," replied Colette. "I thought zat when I got broken, zat would be it, zat I would be no more. But suddenly a wondrous thing occurred. The Red Wings! Surely it happened to you?"

By now Albert didn't know what was real and what wasn't. Or what had or hadn't happened. Colette went on, "It took place so fast zat I can't explain it. You'll have to ask Handyman or one of ze toys zat have returned here more than once."

"Well, who *is* 'Andyman?" Albert quizzed.

"Oh, zat crazy old thing? He's been here since ze beginning, when Kriss Kringle put him here to teach all the broken toys how to repair each other. He can fix anything. He'll even help you become another kind of toy, if you wish—at The Pond."

Albert had so many unanswered questions. The Red Wings? The Pond?

"That's amazing. Is 'Andyman a toy?"

"Why, monsieur, he is ze spirit of ze first toy zat was . . . made when the first cry of a child was heard. Over ze centuries his soul has transformed him into what you see. Ze wisest of all," Colette responded, feeling that this conversation was a waste of her precious time. "I don't know why I am telling you zese things. First time here or not, you are a toy, and you know zis to be true."

"But, I'm not . . . ."

"Zat is enough of zat talk," she said, cutting him off with a wave of her hand.

But Albert pressed, "May I please ask *one* more question?"

"No, no, no. Now I must dance!" she replied and moved over to crank the handle of her music box.

"I'm sorry to have bothered you," said Albert. "I'll be on me way." He turned to leave just as Colette realized how unkind she had been.

"No, wait," she pleaded. "Please do not go. I am sorry. I spoke so rudely. I have been silent for so long zat I have forgotten my manners. *S'il vous plaît*, forgive me, monsieur. Please?"

Albert smiled and walked back to the lovely ballerina.

"It is nice to be able to speak, especially to one like you," she continued. "And I will answer all your questions."

Albert had made a new friend. It was the first time in days he had felt some happiness.

"As an apology for my behavior, let me dance zis dance for you. It will be my special gift to you . . . ?" Colette stopped. "Why, monsieur, you have not told me your name."

"Albert, ma'am," he replied.

Colette moved back to the handle and cranked it a few times. It began to turn by itself. The Forest was filled with the haunting melody of the ancient lullaby.

Albert suddenly became frightened and reached up to stop the handle from turning. "The Broken Army! They might 'ear your music. Aren't you frightened?"

"Broken Army? Frightened of what?" she laughed.

"Then you don't know?"

"I know zat there is nothing to fear in Kriss Kringle's sack," she answered and instructed the reluctant boy to turn the crank again. Albert tried to protest but Colette insisted. With one great pull on the crank, Albert started the handle turning around and around. Once again the music played.

"Zis will be *our* dance, Monsieur Albert. A dance of friendship."

She then took her place at the center and, with the joyous sounds resonating throughout The Forest, she began to pirouette—the mirrored lid reflecting her every movement.

Albert stepped back in admiration. She was right. She was truly a work of art. Enrapt with her dance, Albert did not notice certain movements in The Forest.

Without warning there was yelling and shouting. A division of the soldiers seen earlier had discovered them and, before Albert could react, one of them grabbed Colette and carried her screaming into The Forest.

"Albert! *Mon petit* Albert!" cried the terrified dancer. But quickly Colette's screams faded as she was carried deeper and deeper into The Forest.

Albert made a mad dash after her, but the Grablies had wheels and sped swiftly away with their prisoner.

At once, many of the broken toys converged on the frightened boy. They grabbed, poked, and prodded, trying to capture him.

"Leave me alone!" screamed the angry boy. His shouts momentarily confused them, for none of the other toys they had seized had offered this much resistance. They stopped their clanging and sputtering long enough for him to break free and run.

Now somewhat recovered, they continued their pursuit. But with their various parts missing, they only managed to crash into each other, and fell into a large heap on the ground.

The racket of their arguing faded as Albert raced to safety. He was free!

Suddenly, two black arms came from nowhere and grabbed him.

CHAPTER ELEVEN

The Understanding

TERRIFIED, THE BOY SLOWLY turned to find Deliah smiling at him.

"I thought you might need some help, honey," she said kindly.

Albert was momentarily relieved. But he could still hear the faint sounds of Colette's cries in the distance.

"Albert! Oh, Monsieur Albert! Please help me!" Colette cried.

"I 'ave to go after 'er!" he implored.

"There is nothing you can do for her now," Deliah stated and held him back.

"But we must try!" he insisted.

"The Grablies have her, the poor dear," came the Southern drawl from under the red skirt. "And if we follow them we will surely get broken, too."

"I'm afraid she's right," Deliah seconded. "We are no match for the Army of the Broken Toys."

"This is crazy. 'Ere I am arguing with a flip-flop doll about trying to rescue a ballerina doll. I 'ave just got to get out of this place."

"There is only one way out, honey," said Deliah as she released him.

Desperately he pleaded, "Then please tell me the way."

Deliah looked at Albert and pointed up.

"Up?" he grimaced. "But 'ow can I get up there?"

"Be needed," stated Arabella.

"What does she mean—be needed?"

Deliah, annoyed at Arabella's interrupting, continued, "The only way out of Kriss Kringle's sack is to be needed, to be wanted."

"Let me finish the story, Deliah," pleaded Arabella. "It's my turn."

"Flop!"

"There, that's better," stated Arabella as she fixed her tangled golden hair. "When Kriss Kringle gets to a little boy or girl's home, he just reaches into this sack and tells us which toy he wants. Instantly that toy jumps into his hand," she continued. "So you see, you *must* be wanted and needed to leave here."

"I bet I could just cut me way out of 'ere!" said the streetwise Albert.

Arabella and Deliah both started laughing.

"This is a magic sack, Albert," Arabella said sweetly. "It may look small from the outside, but in here there are no boundaries. You could walk forever and never reach the end."

"You can't cut what you can't touch, little boy," said Horseradish as he came from behind a large cog where he had been eavesdropping.

All were a little startled, fearing it was a Grablie.

"Oh, dear me! Horseradish! It's only you!" Arabella exclaimed and began to faint, but Albert caught her arm. She looked up at him and, ever the flirt, smiled.

"We thought you were a Grablie!" Deliah's voice trembled from under the yellow dress.

Albert released the recovered Arabella and returned his attention to Horseradish.

"You called me 'little boy,'" he said. "Does that mean you believe I am a boy?"

At that moment Topp C. came spinning in, once again startling them.

"Oh, now stop this!" Arabella screamed. She removed the fan tied to her waist and began fanning herself. "I can't take any more of these unannounced callers."

> "I am oh so dreadfully sorry, I say,
> "But I wasn't trying to scare you away,"

Topp C. apologized.

"I guess we are all a bit jumpy," said Albert.

> "We have not been properly introduced.
> "Allow me to correct this abuse,"

Topp C. said and handed Albert his card. It read *Topp C. Turvey—A pleasure to serve ye!*

"And a pleasure to meet you, too, Topp C.," said Albert, extending his hand to the well-dressed top. "I'm Albert, sir, but what does the 'C.' stand for?"

> "Circulus is my middle name;
> "For this my mother takes the blame."

Topp C. took a small bow.

They shook hands and smiled at each other.

"A boy in the sack, I believe,
"Is very hard to conceive,"

continued Topp C.

"But Handyman has explained to us all,
"That indeed this is truly possi-ball."

"Why, suh, you are the very first human who has ever entered this magic sack!" Arabella exclaimed in awe.

"That's great! But 'ow do I become the first 'uman to get out of 'ere?" moaned Albert.

"That is a problem, that's for sure.
"It shall be hard to find a cure,"

considered Topp C.

"If no one out there knows you're here,
"You'll not be asked for, that I fear.
"If no one asks you to appear,
"Then here you must stay, that is clear."

"I don't understand a word you are sayin'!" Albert declared.

Horseradish rocked over and said, "What our rhyming friend is trying to tell you is that unless someone outside the sack asks for you by name, you will remain here forever."

"No way out?" thought Albert. "Oh, Tezzy, what am I going to do?"

"Only Kriss Kringle can help you," said Deliah from her inverted position.

The frustrated Albert blurted out, "Won't someone please tell me who this Kriss Kringle is?"

The toys looked amongst themselves in disbelief.

"Why, everyone knows who he is," stated Horseradish.

"But I don't," Albert answered.

Topp C. spun to the boy and held his monocle just in front of his right eye, trying to get a more focused look.

"You told us your story, oh so glum,
"But where did you say you hailed from?"

"'Ailed from?" Albert repeated. "What does that mean?"

"Where were you born," Deliah whispered from under the skirt.

❄

"Oh. I don't know. I don't know me real folks."
Deliah sighed, "I'm sorry about that."
Impatiently Topp C. said,

> "Now, now, little boy, you are making me crazed.
> "Just answer my question on where you were raised."

"In London, sir," Albert said.

> "Fine, sublime.
> "About time!"

Topp C. stated.

> "Father Christmas is the man that you know,
> "The funny old man who lives in the snow."

"Father Christmas!" exclaimed the elated boy. "That's Kriss Kringle?! You must be jokin', sir."

> "I do not make jokes, my dear sweet lad,
> "For wasting time only makes me mad."

So this was Father Christmas's toy sack! Albert had always wondered how Father Christmas could carry one bag and never have to refill it. Albert was overjoyed at this news.

"Father Christmas is the most wonderful man. 'E'll get me out of 'ere," the boy said confidently.

"In America we call him St. Nicholas," added Arabella.

"Or Santa Claus," piped in Deliah.

"Yes, Albert," whinnied Horseradish, "and in Germany, where I was originally carved, we call him *Weihnachtsman*—or Christmas Man."

"But if he doesn't know you are here, I'm afraid he won't know to ask for you," Arabella added.

"But can't someone please tell 'im I'm 'ere?"

"I'm sorry, Albert," replied Horseradish. "Once we leave this sack, we are just toys—to be played with. We lose our ability to speak and move freely about. There's no way any of us can tell the old man."

"Oh," sighed Albert. "What am I going to do? If Father Christmas can't 'elp me get out, no one can." Suddenly the thought of being trapped in the sack forever terrified the little boy.

"It's not so bad in here, Albert," said Arabella, attempting to cheer him up, for she could sense his pain. "You want for nothing here; whatever your needs, they are fulfilled. And besides," she flirted, "you will always be here to greet me when I return. Isn't that wonderful for you?"

"Oh, Arabella," Horseradish scolded. "Is that all you can think of? Don't worry, Albert. I suppose even a little boy's needs can be provided for."

Albert pondered this for a moment. He realized that he hadn't slept, but he didn't feel sleepy. Nor was he hungry or thirsty, although it must have been hours since he'd last eaten. Maybe even days! He had no idea how long ago he had ventured into the sack seeking warmth from the cold London night.

Albert looked around at the faces of the toys staring back at him. Something had been puzzling him.

"Tell me," he wondered. "Why are we all about the same size? I should be much taller than any of you. After all, I am a boy."

"In this land, we are all equal," Horseradish explained. "No one is greater or lesser than any other."

Abruptly, Horseradish's ears flickered. Noises in the distance! The broken soldiers approaching!

Topp C. yelled,

> "The Grablies! Hide!
> "Horseradish! Ride!"

"Flip!"

"Get us out of here, Deliah!" Arabella screamed from her hiding place under the red skirt. "Please, don't let them break us!"

The small band scrambled in every direction, taking cover behind broken parts.

CHAPTER TWELVE

The Plan

ALBERT AND HIS COMPANIONS watched from their hiding places as the Grablies entered a dingle nearby. They were in luck, for the Army of Broken Toys was on a mission and had no time to look for the pretty ones. They marched through quickly.

> "That was a close one we all know in our hearts.
> "Another few moments, we'd be missing some parts,"

rhymed Topp C., feeling it safe to leave his hiding place.

The others followed.

"Who are they?" asked Albert.

"The enemy," came the muffled Southern drawl. "The Grablies."

"I know that. I've 'eard you call them that," said Albert. "But what are they?"

> "They are the Army of Broken Toys.
> "They are the cause of all this noise,"

stated Topp C., still keeping watch for more soldiers.

"Why do you call them the Grablies?" he questioned further.

"Because when they grab you, they break you apart. You become mean, like them," answered Deliah.

> "Then they take you to follow their leader.
> "No Name's his name and he's the defeater,"

added Topp C.

Poor Albert was so confused by all this; he blurted out, "Why are they trying to 'urt you? What is going on 'ere?"

"We've been asking the same question ourselves," pondered Horseradish.

"You see, Albert, there has never been any turmoil in the sack; that is, until recently," continued Deliah. "Then some strange toy entered, and started forming an army."

"The Army of Broken Toys," added Horseradish.

"Anyway," Deliah continued, "they now live in a giant broken-down old cuckoo clock outside The Forest."

"An army of broken toys? An old clock? A strange toy, the leader?" mumbled Albert, trying to absorb this. "Well, what kind of toy is it?"

"We don't know," said Horseradish. "We just call it what we hear the Army call it—No Name."

"And if we don't stop them," sighed the Southern drawl beneath the red skirt, "there won't be enough toys ready in time for Christmas."

Horseradish continued, "There are only so many *new* toys put in here before the sleigh takes off on Christmas Eve. Most of what he gives away are restored toys like us."

"Kriss Kringle will run out of toys very quickly if we get broken," Arabella added. "There will be no toys to jump into his hand, and all those little children will be so disappointed."

"But this is Father Christmas's sack! That could never 'appen," protested Albert.

> "Dear boy, let me make it crystal clear.
> "We're in danger of no Yuletide cheer,"

piped Topp C., still on watch.

> "If all this continues, it does now appear,
> "That many a child will be shedding a tear.
> "For each precious moment, as Christmas draws near,
> "No toys for Kriss Kringle is what we do fear."

"For you see, once they get inside here, even the new toys are in danger of being broken by the Grablies before Kriss Kringle can deliver them," Horseradish responded.

The thought of a toyless Christmas angered Albert. In his life on the outside, he had never had a lavish Christmas, but even the one or two toys Father Christmas left each year had brought him so much joy.

"Why don't you stop them?" Albert challenged. "Why don't you put up a fight?"

"Fight?" they said to each other quizzically.

"We don't know how to fight," Horseradish stated.

"We are just toys without weapons to fight,
"Though even with weapons, it wouldn't be right.
"The love that we carry is our greatest might.
"How sad for us all if we acted in spite."

"But I saw guns and swords on some of your own tin soldiers," Albert protested. "We could use those!"

"Shame on you, Albert," the toys scolded.

Horseradish moved closer to the boy. "Those are only for play, not to hurt with."

"Just because someone uses them for wrong,
"We don't have to follow and go along,"

said Topp C.

Arabella, still under the red dress, added, "Handyman would never let us return to this magic sack if we hurt anyone."

"Well, you must do something," Albert said as he arose from the building block he was sitting on. "You can't let this 'appen! And we must rescue Colette!"

"What you say, dear boy, is how we feel,
"But what can *we* do to end this ordeal?"

"Let me think," pondered Albert.

"This is quite the silly thing, indeed.
"A human can't help toys to be freed,"

Topp C. said defiantly.

"Quiet!" commanded Horseradish. "Let the boy think."

The toys watched as Albert paced, contemplating the problem. After what seemed like an eternity, he turned to the toys with a confident smile. He had a plan.

"I've got an idea! If they 'ave to break you to make you one of them, then *you* 'ave to fix them to make *them* one of you!"

"That's brilliant!" they all exclaimed.

"By George, you're right, it might just work at that.
"Forget what I said as I tip my hat,"

added Topp C. as he bobbed his hat once.

"Brilliant," said Deliah with a trace of sarcasm. "But how do we do it?"

"Yes, Albert, how do we do it?" questioned the others.

Albert realized he would have to do all the thinking. He resumed pacing back and forth. Until . . .

"I've got it!" Albert said, turning back quietly to the group. "We lead the Broken Army back to 'Andyman's and trap them inside the great machines!"

"Not me!" yelled Arabella, retreating back under the red skirt. "I'm not going anywhere near them!"

"Hush, Arabella! Just listen to him!" warned Deliah.

"We'll paint them! We'll clean them up and paint them!" said Albert. "They fight with weapons; we fight with paintbrushes."

"Paintbrushes! We all know how to use them," Deliah said, her eyes agleam. "Handyman taught us when we were here before."

"But, Albert," questioned Horseradish. "How do we get them to follow us to the workshop?"

"If you ask me," shuddered Arabella, "I think we should just give up the whole idea. If it doesn't work, then we'll really be in trouble!"

"We didn't ask you," declared Deliah. "So just hush your mouth."

> "By George the answer is quite clear.
> "Laughter's the thing to lure them here."

said Topp C.

> "The sound of laughter is something they hate.
> "To the workshop they'll chase us, no debate."

"Good idea, Topp C.," congratulated Albert. "And since you are the fastest one 'ere, you spin back to the workshop. Tell all the toys our plan and make sure they are prepared. We'll lure the Army into our trap."

"Shouldn't we ask Handyman first?" implored the frightened Arabella.

"We don't 'ave time. They've got Colette. She's very delicate. We 'ave to rescue 'er before they break 'er apart! Now Topp C., start spinning!" ordered Albert.

Topp C. began to whirl, faster and faster, until his gyration created a low humming sound around him. He sped toward the workshop, his black top hat bobbing swiftly up and down.

> "Cheerio;
> "Time to go."

"Are you ready?" Albert asked the other toys.

"I'm not," cried Arabella. "This is not play. This could really be dangerous—I might get caught. I must ask Handyman."

"Oh, be quiet, Arabella," yelled Deliah. "It's time you stopped acting like a spoiled crybaby . . . and we stopped acting like cowards."

Arabella's trembling caused Deliah's red skirt to shake violently.

"Ready?" asked Albert. "'Ere goes!"

At his signal, they all started laughing. And as expected, the Grablies changed their course and could be heard marching in their direction. Again, Fanfare led the way with his off-key tooting.

"Now we're in for it. I told you this was a stupid idea," sobbed Arabella.

"Hush and keep laughing!" insisted Deliah.

Then they saw them—Grablies coming from every corner of The Forest. It was time to run.

"Don't let them escape!" ordered Rattles, the tin soldier, when he saw them. "You'll have to answer to No Name if they get away!"

And the chase was on! At least, it was supposed to be. The Broken Army was better at falling than running. And their broken parts kept some of them from traveling in a forward direction.

Rattles, his rusty sword raised, led the advancing Army. He tried to keep his soldiers in formation, but many just couldn't move in a straight line. A one-eyed Teddy bear, named Un-Bear-Able, whose fur was rubbed off by some loving child his last time out, kept losing his wool stuffing and had to stop to restuff himself.

A rainbow-colored bouncing ball bounced a few times and then deflated, forcing the nearest toy to stop and blow him back up. There was much confusion and arguing among the soldiers as they stumbled and fell over each other.

"Hurry up, Dribble," ordered Rattles to the almost deflated ball. "We mustn't let those toys escape."

"S-s-so s-s-sorry, s-s-sir," hissed the nearly flattened Dribble. "I s-s-shall be s-s-successfully s-s-sound s-s-soon."

Rattles ordered Un-Bear-Able to come and reinflate Dribble. While the bear blew into the valve of the ball, Rattles charged on ahead so as not to lose sight of Albert and his companions.

It wasn't difficult for Albert and the small group of toys to stay ahead of the Army. So when Albert stopped to look back, he saw what looked like a funny clown act as the soldiers fell all over each other. Now, he no longer needed to pretend. His laughter was real.

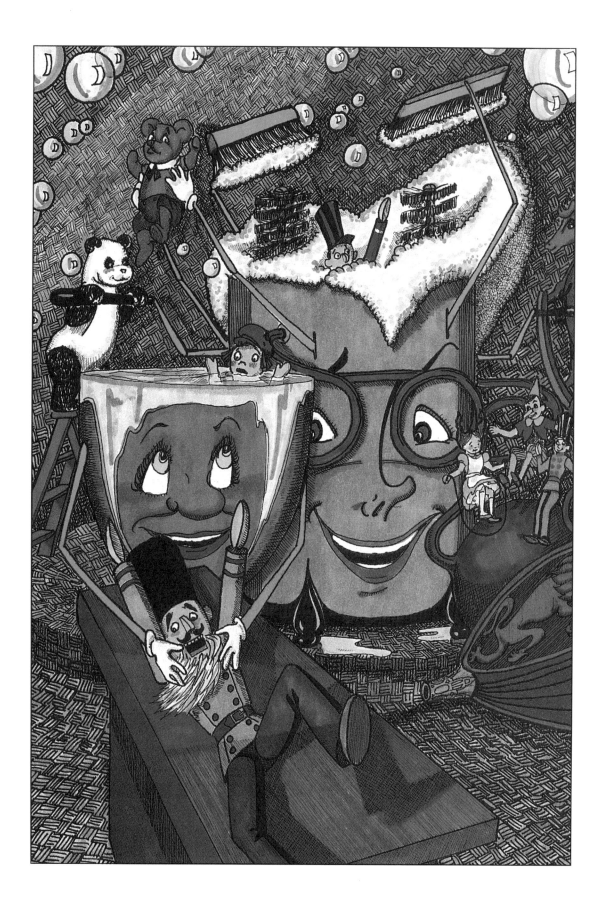

CHAPTER THIRTEEN

The Battle of the Paintbrushes

Topp C. spun into Handyman's workshop calling for all the toys to gather around. Hurriedly, he told them of the plans.

> "So that, my dear friends, is what we must do,
> "If Albert's plans are to be carried through,"

said Topp C., ending the instructions.

Suddenly, Albert, Horseradish, and Deliah-Arabella, still laughing, ran into the workshop well in advance of the Army.

"All right," Albert demanded as he tried to catch his breath, "get those machines going! Everyone get ready!"

All obeyed without hesitating. The giant machines were started and soon began putting out a deafening sound of chugging and clanging. Buckets of paint and brushes were seized. Bolts of cloth were brought in. Needles were threaded. All the toys stood ready as the Army entered the clearing. It was to be a war—the weapons against these paintbrushes.

The toys leaped out and surprised the Broken Army. The Grablies were caught off guard. They had not expected to be challenged. Some of the soldiers were captured and led to the giant cleaning machines. Others were held down while being repainted, glued, or resewn. They were no match for the agile toys.

The warm gust of wind blew and Handyman emerged from his private workshop. The commotion had disturbed his toil and when he saw what was happening he shouted, "No! You fools! Don't do this!"

But it was too late.

Samson, the iron boxer, captured two Grablies: a torn, stuffed blue cat and a broken baby doll. He held the two squirming Grablies, one in each hand, high off the ground while some of the toys expertly repaired their damaged parts. Chutney held a large paintbrush in his trunk and slapped on the finishing touches.

❄

The big black Teddy bear, Un-Bear-Able, jumped Horseradish and attempted to break off one of the rockers.

"Help me!" hollered Horseradish. "Please help me."

Albert ran to his rescue and, after a struggle, managed to pull the bear down just in time.

"Thanks, Albert. I owe you one," Horseradish sighed and he ran to help the others.

"Don't think about it," Albert yelled after him. "Deliah, give me a 'and with the bear!"

Flip-Flop ran over with two giant needles and handed one to Albert. Deliah started pushing the bear's stuffing back into his seams and sewing him back together. Albert worked on replacing the button eye, using the sewing skills Tezzy had once shown him.

"What's going on up there? Is it over yet?" queried the frightened Arabella.

"No," commanded Deliah. "And be still. I can't sew straight with all your commotion."

A whirring sound could be heard as nine brightly colored jacks spun rapidly to form an impenetrable line against the soldiers. As one of the Grablies attacked, it found itself knocked to the ground by the spinning arms of the jacks. Then other toys raced in and restrained the fallen soldier while any necessary repairs were being made.

Finally most of the repairs were finished. Smiling, Albert and Deliah stepped back to admire their handiwork. There was a sense of victory in the air. But no!

Suddenly, a bucket of paint came flying at Albert. He turned just in time to see that it had been thrown by the repaired Un-Bear-Able.

Albert ducked and the paint splattered all over the workshop. The toys froze, staring at each other in confusion.

"But why did that toy do what he did do,
"For now he's all sewn, painted, shiny, and new?"

interrogated Topp C.

"Run, run!" yelled Handyman. "Run to stay whole!"

The plan had not worked! The newly repaired soldiers were still fighting the toys. And now because they had been mended, they could run and fight without falling. The plan not only failed, but it had backfired!

The toys ran screaming into the protection of The Forest, followed closely by the angry soldiers.

"Halt!" yelled Rattles to his troops. "Let them go for now. We shall stay here and finish repairing ourselves. Then there will be no way they can escape us."

Obediently, the troops stopped their chase and returned to the great racket of the machines operating at full steam.

"No Name will be so pleased with me," gloated Rattles softly to himself.

CHAPTER FOURTEEN

The Secret

THE SOUND OF THE MACHINERY wafted throughout The Forest as the panicked toys ran to find new hiding places. Faintly, the voice of Rattles filtered through and Albert stopped to listen.

"Thank you, my friends. We all thank you, you foolish toys!"

Albert was stunned. What had he done wrong? He had to find Handyman. He ran to find the others. Maybe they knew where he was.

He ran for what seemed a long time. Finally winded and confused, he caught up with the toys. But no one knew where the old creature was. No one had even seen him since they left the workshop. And they wanted to find him, too, so they spread out to search.

"Handyman, where are you?" they called out.

A gentle warm breeze made its way into the glen and magically, Handyman appeared to their calls.

"My poor, innocent little toys," he addressed the startled group. "What have you done?"

The toys, exhausted from their fighting and running, began to weep. Albert approached Handyman to apologize. It had been his plan and he would take all the blame.

"You don't need to say it, Albert. I know you are sorry," he said compassionately. "But you must learn to ask before taking on such a grand responsibility."

"Oh, 'Andyman," sobbed Albert. "What 'ave I done? I was so sure that by makin' them whole, fixing them up, they would be like the rest of you."

"Albert, my dear little boy, being broken or not being pretty doesn't make someone strange or evil," said Handyman. "It's our hearts and souls that make us so."

Albert looked up at him.

❋

"Didn't you notice something else unusual about the Army other than their broken parts?" asked the creature.

Albert shook his head. So much had happened so quickly, he hadn't had time to notice much of anything.

"I did!" yelled Deliah. "None of them smiled!"

"That's right, my little friends," Handyman replied. "They have no smiles."

"I don't understand," said Albert.

The eclectic array of toys gathered around, for they, too, didn't understand. At the rear of the group, a strange blue patchwork cat with a wide grin listened.

"I am known by all of you as the fixer of toys," Handyman continued. "I have yet another job that you know nothing about. I am the keeper of smiles."

"The keeper of the smiles, oh my, you do say?
"That is a new one on us today,"

Topp C. said.

"What kind of a job is that?" asked Horseradish.

From under the red skirt, Arabella drawled, "Dear me, whatever are you talking about?"

Handyman turned his back to the toys. A hush fell over the group. Again the gentle breeze blew into the glen, but stopped when he turned around to look at their faces.

Clasping his ten hands together, he began in his old rumbling voice, "When each of you is out in the human world and a child loves and plays with you, you have a warm loving feeling inside. A happy smile is on your face and in your heart.

"But then one day the inevitable happens. No matter how carefully you are handled or how much love you are given, you get broken. Perhaps in an accident, or maybe in a fit of anger. But no matter, you get broken. Then you are unwanted and you lose your happy smile."

Some of the toys began to sob as they remembered the children who had once loved them but did no longer. Others remained very still and listened. Albert watched Handyman intently, thinking that this loving, blue-haired creature reminded him of someone he had once known.

"As you are finding your way back to this magic sack of dreams," Handyman continued, "there is a sadness in your hearts. A longing to belong. To be needed. To be loved."

All of the toys knew this to be true, even the boy, Albert.

"But when we come back and fall through the circle of light in the kaleidoscope," interrupted Horseradish, fighting back his tears, "we always feel happy. We smile again."

"Exactly," agreed Handyman, "because your smile has flown back here ahead of you and eagerly awaits your return. As soon as you leave the snowflake of the kaleidoscope, it flies into your heart and you smile again. No matter what changes we do to you on the outside, even if you dive into The Pond, you always have the same soul. Your smile knows you always."

Again the mention of The Pond, observed Albert. But somehow this didn't seem the time to ask about it.

Chutney, the elephant, spoke up. "Goodness to gracious. Be so good as to be telling us why the soldiers are without their smiles."

Handyman continued sadly, "A short time ago, a broken and very angry toy came inside. He was so bitter and mean that even his smile would not stick."

"Who is the toy?" asked Horseradish. "You know *all* the toys that have ever been here."

"I'm sorry," said Handyman wearily, "but I feel that this is a new toy to the sack. This is its first time here. But even if it were not so, this toy's intense anger and hatred would make him unrecognizable, even to me."

Bree-Zing, a brightly painted lady dragon kite, flew out of the group. She sailed close to Handyman.

"How do you know it's a toy, sir?" inquired the kite.

"Maybe it's another boy—like Albert," offered Horseradish.

"No, it is a toy. Of that I am sure. I sense that I know its maker," added Handyman very softly—and somewhat mysteriously. Then he turned his attention back to the gathering and continued, "Until you manage to find your way back here, your smiles await you in a great golden chest that sits at the foot of the kaleidoscope."

"I've never seen it," said Deliah.

"No," responded Handyman. "It was my secret until the chest was stolen by this angry toy and taken to the great cuckoo clock. Somehow, it must have locked the smiles inside. For they surely would have flown back to me."

"Are all the smiles locked up there?" inquired Horseradish.

"Not quite," said Handyman, signaling for them to be very quiet. "I am about to show you something no one but myself has ever seen. But you must each remain very still and silent."

The toys watched with great expectation and Handyman reached into one of his pockets. Not finding what he was looking for, he checked another of his many pockets with a different hand.

"Now, where did I put it?" he mumbled to himself.

All ten of his hands frantically searched his pockets. Still there was nothing. Where was it? Handyman began pacing, trying to remember.

"I know you are in here somewhere," the confused creature muttered.

Albert was finding it difficult to keep from laughing at Handyman's confusion. But the others were watching with great concern, so he remained silent.

Then it dawned on Handyman. Using all ten hands to unbutton his coat, each pair of hands taking one button, he opened one side of his coat to reveal a hidden pocket!

"There you are, you little rascal," he said with a smile, reaching inside and slowly pulling out a shining gold pouch which he placed in another of his hands. "Now watch."

With a different pair of hands, he untied the two drawstrings. Using still two more of his hands, he opened the pouch. Everyone heard a giggling sound and then, as if a Roman candle had been ignited, a ball of golden light shot into the air, momentarily blinding the toys. But strangely, it did not hurt their eyes. Instead, a great laughter erupted from the light.

The laughter was infectious and soon all the toys were laughing. Instantly they forgot their troubles and began to dance, some by themselves, some in a circle with others. Deliah-Arabella flipped and flopped over and over with joy. The laughter was so powerful even the great Handyman was forced to laugh.

The golden light flew off into The Forest with great speed, but soon returned to the gathering. It flew to each of them, pausing only for a moment in front of each of their faces—even Albert's. Then it flew to Handyman and began to flicker and grow dim.

The gaiety which all had felt began to fade. The dancing stopped; the laughter died down. Confused, the toys turned to watch the dimming glow.

"No, he's not here, my lonely friend," said Handyman as he raised the open shining gold pouch. "Come back to rest."

The flickering light wearily flew back into the pouch, stopping momentarily at the opening. Then it dropped inside. Handyman drew the strings together, tied them, and placed the golden pouch into the large hidden pocket.

The laughter had subsided completely, and the toys looked as if they were coming out of a trance.

"What was that?" questioned Arabella in wonder and disbelief.

"It was a smile," Handyman said simply. "No Name's smile. And it was looking for its owner, hoping to be accepted this time. It was saddened when it couldn't find him among you, so it came back to the pouch to rest."

The group was silent a long while.

> "That is why the new paint and clothes,
> "Did not work with the plan we chose,"

announced Topp C., breaking the silence.

"Yes, Topp C.," said Handyman sadly. "It's what is *on the inside* that matters. And unless the Grablies get their smiles back, they will never be free."

"And Kriss Kringle won't have enough toys to give out this Christmas," lamented Arabella.

"Can't you fix this, Handyman?" shouted Bree-Zing, fluttering overhead. "You can fix anything."

The toys hurrahed in agreement.

"This has never happened before," confessed the old creature. "I have no powers in this matter."

The toys were shocked! There was something the great Handyman couldn't fix! He had always been able to repair every problem. Suddenly, they felt helpless.

Even Bree-Zing found it difficult to stay airborne, so she glided to the ground.

Depression swept through the gathering, for they could see no way out of this dilemma.

"Well, you 'ave to do somethin'," demanded Albert. "*I* may be stuck in this 'ere old sack forever, but there are lots of children outside who are goin' to be very sad if nothin' is done."

Then with commitment he continued, "Sometimes you 'ave to fight for what's yours or the people that you love could get hurt. Back in London I used to battle Kettle and Smudge to keep what was mine if me Tezzy and I was to eat."

> "Dear boy, a mess of things you already have made.
> "Better off we'd be, if at the workshop we'd stayed,"

snapped Topp C.

"At least *he* did something!" declared Arabella and took his arm in hers. "My good toys, we must take some action."

Deliah poked her head from under the yellow dress, and said with a sly smile, "Now you're learning."

"I must confess, Albert may be our only hope, at that," shrugged Handyman, turning to the boy. "So, young man, our destiny is in your *two* hands."

CHAPTER FIFTEEN

The Jacks

ALL EYES WENT TO ALBERT, who was pacing. The toys watched in hopeful silence. After a few minutes, Albert turned to them.

"First, we 'ave to get inside the clock to find out what's going on. We need to know more about the Grablies."

The toys shuddered at the thought of going inside the cuckoo clock.

"But how will we get in?" asked Horseradish.

"We must infiltrate their Army. We'll need a spy," responded Albert. "Now that the toys 'ave repaired themselves, they won't be able to tell who's a soldier and who's not."

"Since you all look the same, you would blend right in with them," agreed Handyman.

The blue cat, which had stayed at the back of the group, quietly slipped into The Forest, unnoticed.

"Except," said Arabella, "we smile and laugh and they don't."

"Right, Arabella," added Albert, "but whoever goes in must pretend to be sad. 'E'll never get caught as long as 'e doesn't smile or laugh."

"Flip!"

"I'll go," volunteered Deliah.

All the toys cheered.

"Flop!"

"Oh, no you don't!" screamed Arabella. "You're not dragging me in there! I said *we* had to take action, not *I*!"

"Leave it to Miss Priss to stop Deliah," whispered Molly, the rag doll, into Horseradish's ear.

"Handyman, can't you separate the two of us?" begged Arabella. "Please?!"

"I'm afraid no, my silly Arabella," replied Handyman. "You two are one and the same, each a different part of the whole."

Confused, Arabella questioned, "What does that mean?"

"It means that where I go, you go, honey," laughed Deliah.

"But how will they get in, my boy,
"Even if they mask their joy?"

asked Topp C.

"The place I hear is dangerous.
"The guards they say, cantankerous."

"Flip!"

"Oh, no," moaned Arabella as she pulled the red skirt over herself.

The shiny brown metallic jack that Albert had seen earlier came spinning over. He was wearing a large ten-gallon cowboy hat on his pointed head and a red checked scarf tied around his neck.

Albert could see that it was a jack just like the ones little girls played with on the sidewalks of London. They would toss a small red ball into the air and have to grab some of the ten jacks before the ball bounced twice.

"Excuse me, pardner, I don't mean to be no bother," ventured the jack, "but my name is Flap Jack and I was wonderin' if me and my brothers could be of any assistance?"

At that moment the eight other jacks twirled their way through the crowd and spun close to Handyman and Albert. It was quite a sight indeed! For each was a different shiny color and, as they spun, the light reflected off their metal figures, causing the immediate area to shimmer in colored lights. It was a beautiful vision.

"Allow me to introduce my brothers," Flap Jack said and removed his ten-gallon hat.

"Jack Rabbit," he hollered. "Get on up here and say 'howdy' to this here buckaroo."

A bright pink jack spun swiftly to Albert and spoke rapidly. "We don't have much time. We have to act quickly. Let's get a move on! Let's get a move on! Hop! Hop! Hop!"

A cherry red jack rotated in next. Nervously, it looked around and removed its tattered stocking cap. "I'm Jack Knife and don't you forget it! I've been playing on the streets a long time, so I can handle *any* situation."

"Nice to meet you," Albert responded cautiously.

"Don't pay any attention to him. He's just a big bully," effused a gold jack as he gyrated over. But to Albert's surprise the jack didn't stop. Instead he spun circles around the boy and Handyman, his long purple paisley silk scarf trailing after him.

Finally he ceased spinning and said, "My name is Jack-a-Dandy."

Holding out one of his four white-gloved hands for Albert to shake, he glared at Jack Knife. "You must forgive some of my brothers for their lack of class and breeding."

Jack Knife grunted.

Suddenly, an orange jack with triangular eyes and a ragged mouth spun around Arabella.

"Ooooh," he chanted ghostlike while circling the doll.

"Flip!"

Arabella retreated in fear.

Then stopping he said ghoulishly, "I hear stories that the ancient cuckoo clock is haunted."

Arabella began to shake violently under the skirt.

Deliah protested, "Now stop that, Jack-O'-Lantern. It's not nice to go around scaring folks, not even Arabella."

Arabella cautiously poked her head out to protest, but Jack-O'-Lantern leaned down and yelled, "Boo," which of course frightened her again into retreating.

Jack-O'-Lantern's laughter was cut short when Handyman stepped forward and scolded, "That's quite enough of that, my mischievous metallic friend. Go haunt your brothers."

"Yes, sir," responded Jack-O'-Lantern respectfully.

"I apologize for my brothers' behavior," braved the meek voice of an ebony jack. A bright yellow stripe down his back branded him a coward. As he spun slowly forward, Albert could see each of his four arms was yellow-striped as well.

"My name is Jackal," said he timidly, "and I think we should all just run away from here."

Arabella, hearing Jackal's opinion, revealed her smiling face in agreement. But Jack-O'-Lantern sneaked up behind Jackal and grabbed him, yelling, "Gotcha!"

The terrified jack broke free and spun rapidly into The Forest and out of sight.

"I'll not warn you again," bellowed Handyman. "There is much to be done and so little time. If you won't behave yourself, you shall not be allowed to leave the sack this Christmas and must wait until next."

Then a sadness fell over the old creature as he realized what he had said. "That is, of course, if any of you are able to leave—ever."

"I'm sorry, Handyman," Jack-O'-Lantern apologized as he rejoined his brothers. "I promise to behave."

"I'll lay you ten to one that we all make it out this year," wagered Black Jack, the shiny black gambler. "I'll bet those old Grablies will be no match for Albert here."

"I do 'ope you're right," replied Albert, "but we 'ave much to do, lads."

"I'll place a side bet that me and my brothers are gonna be very helpful," Black Jack stated confidently. "Deal us in."

Now the gathering felt better after hearing this fast-talking jack, and they began to rally.

"Are we going to help Albert?" challenged Black Jack.

There came a weak, "Yeah," from a few of the toys.

Disappointed by their response, Black Jack yelled, "I can't hear you."

The toys scrambled to their upright positions.

"Are we going to help the boy?" he boomed.

Their answer was a resounding, unanimous, "Yessss!!"

Albert, touched by their response, was also frightened by the enormous responsibility. The thought that Father Christmas's mission depended on him was overwhelming.

"That's right, mate," said the white jack in a charming Australian accent as he reeled closer to the boy. "We'll do all we must in order to help you."

"Thank you," said Albert. "May I please know your name?"

"Jack-A-Roo, mate," said the shepherd proudly. He was the snowy color of many of the sheep that are tended by his namesake. He removed his bush hat and added, "G'day mate, glad to have you with us."

"That goes for me, too," responded the multicolored jack. One of his arms was red, one green, one yellow, and one blue. His head was purple and his pointed leg was maroon. "They call me Jack-Of-All-Trades," he exclaimed. "Master of none, some say," he chuckled, "but I'll do all that I can."

Albert thanked the nine of them again.

Flap Jack sauntered forward to say, "Pardner, trapped inside that old clock is our sister, Jackaranda. That filly's as purple as the flowers on the South American tree she takes her name from."

"With a fiery Latin temper to match," added Jack-A-Roo, "but we still love her anyway, mate."

"The Grablies caught the poor dear when she came through the kaleidoscope," Jack-a-Dandy spoke up. "We'll do anything to set her free."

Jackal, the meek one, crept back into the glen and added softly, "We fight all the time but that doesn't mean we don't love each other. We are a set. A family."

❄

"We can do and say anything we want to each other," snorted Jack Knife, "but just let an outsider hurt any one of my family and he'll have to answer to me!"

Jack-Of-All-Trades reminded, "Handyman said he could replace Jack-aranda so that we would be a complete set of ten and be able to leave the sack."

"But," interrupted Jack-O'-Lantern, "we won't go without our purple sister. We wouldn't want to frighten her by leaving her alone."

"Hop! Hop! Hop!" insisted Jack Rabbit. "Time's a-wasting. Time's a-wasting. We have to make a move! Albert will solve this quickly. Won't you, Albert?"

"I'll try me best," replied the boy.

"We're betting on you. Aren't we toys?" added Black Jack.

The toys hurrahed enthusiastically.

But Albert looked to Handyman. They exchanged a worried glance, for they knew there was much danger ahead.

Quieting the group down, Handyman spoke. "We must all now listen to Albert's plan."

The toys pushed in very close as the boy carefully outlined his strategy on how they were to get Deliah and Arabella inside the ancient cuckoo clock.

Throughout, the very frightened voice of Arabella could be heard lamenting under the red skirt, "Why me? Why me?"

CHAPTER SIXTEEN

The Fortress

THE ANTIQUATED CUCKOO CLOCK was ornate, but in need of much repair. Several of its large Roman numerals had fallen off. The hour hand spun rapidly in one direction while the minute hand went in the other, sometimes both reversing their directions abruptly. It had been quite grand in its day. Its dark wood was heavily carved with grape clusters and leaves around its sides; animal heads adorned the front. Its pendulum had broken off and the two lead pinecone weights were tangled in a mass of gnarled chain.

The newly repaired Army had just returned to the great clock. The freshly painted soldiers, dragging the screaming Colette with them, were precision marching. Suddenly the small door at the top of the clock sprang open and out flew a strange black bird. Its shrieking sound was more like a vulture than the cuckoo it was supposed to be. The bright red feathers on the underside of its wings matched the fiery blood-red of its angry eyes. Its long black beak curved down to a razor-sharp point.

"Akkkk! It's about time you got back, you pieces of junk!!" The bird's eyes glowed with excitement when he caught the sight of Colette. "I see you have brought me a playmate. Haul her up to my nest so we can get better acquainted. Akkkk! Akkkk!"

The animal heads on the clock came to life, tossing their heads and snorting their approval.

But not one of the Army reacted for they'd heard its ranting before. But the bird terrified Colette. So horrified was she by the creature's pecking and clawing that she momentarily stopped her screaming. She would surely be torn to shreds if the bird got its talons on her. Then there was the clock's ominous entrance, its pitch-black opening hiding unimaginable dangers lurking just inside. She renewed her kicking and screaming, but there was no hope for escape.

❋

"Nom d'un chien, you common rogues," screamed the French dancer. "Put me down!"

Albert, Horseradish, Topp C., and the flip-flop doll, hiding behind a piece of a fire engine, watched her valiant struggle.

"Get her inside quickly," commanded Rattles, waving his shiny sword. "As soon as we take her smile, she'll be one of us. That constant yelling is driving me mad."

"Akkkk! Yes, do bring the pretty one inside," leered the cuckoo.

Suddenly an evil-looking jester marionette swung into the entranceway. The dangling puppet's strings sizzled. Dressed in a torn silver outfit and a three-pointed cap with a bell on each tip, he announced in a loud menacing voice, "All hail! His Grace is coming! All bow to our great leader!"

Albert could see the Army visibly shudder as they dropped to their knees, heads bowed.

"Long live No Name!" they chanted over and over.

Fanfare heralded the Master's arrival with a loud off-key flourish.

Colette was pulled down to the ground by Un-Bear-Able, but still she struggled to be free. Then the sight of an ominous figure towering over the jester paralyzed her.

The figure was covered from head to toe with a flowing red cape. Its green face was darkly shadowed by the cape's hood, but its fierce eyes pierced the blackness. The look of hatred burning in them evidenced many years of pain. The gloved right hand manipulated the control sticks of the jester puppet. As this hooded figure emerged it bobbed slightly up and down. This was No Name.

Colette screamed at the sight.

"Silence!" the jester's voice boomed out.

The Army stopped their chanting, but remained kneeling as if a giant hand were holding them down.

"What is all this racket? The Master wants to know," he continued speaking as the voice of his Master, who was wielding his strings.

No one dared answer but Colette, who, gathering all her courage, challenged the ominous leader.

"Monsieur, or whatever *thing* you are, how dare you toynap me from my music box!" she roared as she pulled away from her captors and headed for the leader. "Who do you think you are? I shall not be treated so rudely!!"

But before she could get too close to No Name, Rattles recaptured her.

"Shall I proceed with the smile removal, Your Greatness?" he asked with nasty anticipation.

No Name's eyes pierced Colette. Then something strange happened. For a brief moment, the hatred appeared to give way to a kind of knowingness.

"Well? Shall I snatch her smile?" badgered Rattles impatiently.

"He heard you the first time!" sneered the jester.

Rattles backed away. No one questioned this new leader whose authority was absolute.

Colette continued to stare defiantly at No Name and he at her. Again, the anger in his eyes seemed to waver. It was not like him to be so indecisive, and the soldiers began to grow restless.

"No Name says . . ." the jester began, but on his own stopped abruptly and in confusion looked up at his Master.

"What was No Name doing? Did he really want me to say that?! Surely he can't mean what he wants me to say," the jester thought to himself.

But No Name had tired of the jester's long pause signifying disobedience. He pulled his servant's strings sharply, causing the puppet to jerk into the air.

Obediently, the bewildered jester spoke as ordered. "No Name says 'No. Leave her smile alone.'"

The Army was stunned, and muttered their disapproval.

"Silence! You fools!" shouted the jester. "Just take her to the Hall of Greatness."

"Akkkk! Yes, drag her on in. I'll make her feel welcome. Akkkk! Akkkk!" shrieked the flapping beast as it backed into its nest and slammed the door.

No Name turned, sweeping his cape grandly, and reentered the clock, bobbing up and down and pulling the dangling jester behind him. Rattles followed them, pushing Colette forward. Lastly, the disgruntled troops began to enter in formation.

Albert and his friends looked at each other in disbelief.

"So that's No Name," declared Horseradish. "No wonder things are so bad here."

"At least Colette kept her smile," said Deliah.

"For now," added Horseradish.

"I just hope I'll be able to keep mine," grumbled Arabella from underneath.

CHAPTER SEVENTEEN

The Queen

"This must be stopped, please believe.
"It's imperative that I leave,
"For soon it will be Christmas Eve,"

whispered Topp C.

"Imperative?" inquired Albert, for he did not understand the word.

"Yes, necessary, must be done.
"My time here should not have begun."

"That's what Colette said, too," Albert mused. "It seems this is all a mistake. For me, for you, for everyone."

Horseradish spoke up. "Why, Topp C.? Why shouldn't you be here?"

"My days of play were hardly finished.
"The dreams in me were undiminished."

stated Topp C.

The toys began to understand, but Albert had no idea what the top was talking about.

"I was broken on the outside.
"My windup spring, I must confide,
"Looked like a knot that had been tied.

"The children really didn't care,
"To them I needed no repair.
"With their hands I spun anywhere."

"Did they still love you, Topp C., even though you were broken?" asked the puzzled Albert.

Trying to keep a stiff upper lip, the top explained,

"The adults could never see the dreams,
"The fantasies and the childhood schemes.
"All to them was only as it seems.

"The children couldn't love me less,
"Although my paint was quite a mess,
"For friend I was in their caress.

"Imagination is so pure.
"Dented metal it will obscure,
"For love and friendship do endure."

"Well, if there was so much love and you were needed, why did you return here?" challenged the boy.

Topp C.'s monocle misted over as he explained,

"As the children slept, adults crept in,
"My journey's end was a foul tin—
"Imagine me in a rubbish bin."

Albert looked at the genteel toy. "I bet the little boy that played with you the most cried and threw a fit when 'e discovered you missing the next day."

Topp C. laughed.

"Would serve those sightless grownups right,
"For Tom could put up quite a fight.
"When anger struck, 'twas quite a sight."

The image of the dapper Topp C. lying in a garbage can made Albert chuckle. Then he peered out from behind the fire engine and determined that it was time to take action.

"Are you ready, everyone?" he whispered.

"Ready as I'll ever be," came Arabella's weak reply.

"You just give us the cue,
"And our tasks we will do,"

stated Topp C.

But then the top touched Albert's shoulders and warned,

"Once you are broken, we can't repair.
"A child's life is fragile, so beware."

Albert tried to smile, but couldn't.

As the last of the troops were entering the clock, Albert gave the signal. Topp C. went whirling out into the clearing followed by Albert astride Horseradish, all laughing and singing.

"Yoohoo!" taunted Albert. "Catch us if you can!"

"Look!" hollered the last soldier in line. "Three pretty toys! Let's get them!"

"Want to play tag?" challenged Horseradish.

A group of soldiers did an about-face and ran from the clock in pursuit.

> "To play this game we've seen fit,
> "To start if off, you'll be *it!*"

teased Topp C. as he tipped his hat.

Albert and Horseradish ran one way while Topp C. spun off in another to divide their pursuers.

Rattles emerged from the clock to see what was delaying his soldiers. When he saw the toys running toward The Forest, he shouted, "I always did like a good game of hide-'n-seek!"

During all this commotion, no one noticed Deliah, faking her frown, come from her hiding place to join in the chase. Her frown enabled her to blend right in with the troops.

From upside down, Arabella pleaded, "Please, Deliah, don't smile!"

"Don't worry. I find absolutely nothing amusing about any of this," whispered Deliah. "Now hush up!"

"Hey, you!" barked Rattles.

Deliah spun around. The tin soldier was pointing directly at her. She had been found out!

"Soldier, I'm talking to you," snarled Rattles, annoyed at her silence.

Could it be that she had been accepted? Hadn't he called her "soldier"? Gathering up all her courage, she snapped to attention.

"Yes, sir!" she replied crisply.

"There are already enough soldiers following those pretty ones; so I want you to march to the Hall of Greatness and receive No Name's orders," commanded Rattles.

"Yes, sir," answered the relieved doll.

Rattles marched ahead into the clock. Deliah followed. Flip-Flop had made it inside!

Suddenly Deliah stumbled. "Ow! Fiddly bob! There goes another nail," cried Arabella.

Deliah slapped the front of her skirt and whispered, "Shhhh!"

Loneliness permeated this musty old timepiece. Its giant cogs were decaying, and large cracks in the walls permitted only slivers of light to enter, casting ghostly shadows through the dusty air. Without warning, the great cogs and springs began to move, giving an eerie life to this forbidding fortress. Then, just as suddenly, the tick-tock-ticking stopped, and all was silent—for awhile.

Deliah cued up with the main Army just as they entered the Hall of Greatness. Looking around, Deliah guessed that this space might have been a storage area where humans hid secret letters or valuables.

No Name sat on a large throne which was draped with royal blue fabric. A single shaft of light, pouring through a crack, illuminated him. The jester, manipulated by this mysterious dictator, faced the arriving soldiers.

For the first time, a shudder of fear swept through Deliah, so strong that even Arabella felt it.

"No Name is very pleased that you have repaired yourselves," commended the jester. "You are now better able to serve him."

The soldiers cheered. Rattles knew he had gained favors. Fanfare began to trumpet his own off-key salute. The noise was so deafening that the soldiers covered their ears.

The puppet screamed above the din, "Will somebody please take that dented pile of junk back to the workshop and have him hammered out, polished, and tuned!"

Rattles silenced the trumpet by tossing an old rag into the large round opening of the tarnished horn and stepped forward. "Sorry, Your Grace. We were in such a hurry to get back here, we forgot to fix Fanfare."

Rattles snapped his metallic fingers and a soldier quickly ushered the trembling horn out of the clock for repairs.

"As I was saying, No Name is pleased with your progress," said the jester, "but you have not brought in enough prisoners. Christmas Eve is almost here and there is so much work to be done. There are still many smiling toys running free in The Forest. We must make *sure* there are no happy children this Christmas!"

They cheered once again, knowing it would appease their leader.

"But why?" Colette spoke bravely. "Why do you want to hurt all those children? What have they *ever* done to you?"

"Silence, dancer!" commanded the jester. "The Master says that is no business of yours!"

Turning back to the troops, the jester continued, "It has occurred to His Greatness that he needs more tin soldiers like Rattles, his trusted general. With an army of tin soldiers he would be invincible!"

At this compliment, Rattles snapped to attention.

"He commands," continued the puppet, "all who have been without change for at least a century to march directly to The Pond of I-Wish-I-Were."

The soldiers looked sadly to each other. Would this nightmare ever be over? None wanted to change, except Un-Bear-Able. He liked everything about soldiering.

"All right, you piles of junk, line up!" commanded Rattles.

About a fourth of the motley Army cued up behind Un-Bear-Able and prepared to march out.

"And remember," added the jester, "you are not to return to the Hall of Greatness until you have all been transformed into tin soldiers."

"Yes, sir," the troops responded glumly.

"Un-Bear-Able, lead this group of useless rubbish to The Pond. If any can't make the transformation, break them," sneered Rattles.

The ambitious Teddy bear stepped forward. "Yes, sir!" he responded enthusiastically, for becoming a tin soldier might enable him to be a general one day, too.

"March!" ordered Rattles.

Un-Bear-Able led the unit out of the hall. The precision of their marching caused the clock to shake.

Colette waited until the last soldier exited before turning back to No Name.

"*Pardonnez moi*, monsieur, just what are you going to do with me?" she asked defiantly. "Change me into a tin soldier, too?"

No Name stared at the beautiful ballerina, his eyes transfixed. Long moments passed before the jester spoke. "You are to remain here as our prisoner. No Name decrees that you are to become his queen."

The thought of being queen to this maniac repulsed her. "Does your master think he can pull *my* strings, too?" she laughed derisively.

"Silence! Laughter is forbidden here."

She decided it was better to hold her tongue and to plan her escape.

Meanwhile, as prearranged, Albert and Horseradish rendezvoused with Topp C. at the dollhouse where they could safely hide.

CHAPTER EIGHTEEN

The Challenge

AT THAT MOMENT, FROM ANOTHER chamber in the clock, a purple blur came spinning into the Hall of Greatness.

Dribble, the rainbow-colored ball standing next to Deliah, leaned over and whispered, "S-s-surely s-s-she s-s-shall s-s-squelch the s-s-smiling ballerina s-s-swiftly."

"What is the ball talking about?" Deliah thought. But she was too frightened to respond and continued to stand at attention.

The answer to her question was not long in coming. The purple blur circled Colette three times, startling her. As it began to slow down, Deliah recognized Jackaranda, the purple South American jack.

As she stopped twirling, Jackaranda lashed out in a Latin accent, "No! No! No! No! How dare you offer to crown this smiling toe dancer. You promised me that I would be queen, no?!!"

Her turban, piled high with bananas, pineapples, grapes, and other assorted wax fruit, trembled in her fury.

Afraid of what the fiery Latin might do next, the puppet spoke cautiously. "Things have changed. All is not as it was."

In a tirade, the jack started spinning rapidly around and around the hall. Jackaranda was mad!! The soldiers scattered to get out of her way. Then she again taunted Colette by spinning circles around her.

"Stop this at once," mouthed the marionette for his master. "No Name is displeased."

Not one to give up, Jackaranda countered, "Then let us spin to prove who should be queen. We shall have a contest," she hissed. "The dance of the queens."

No Name wasn't listening. His attention was on Colette and he stared deeply into her eyes.

Jackaranda noticed the special look that the Master was giving the ballerina.

❄

Angrily, she let out a long mournful cry and began to spin rapidly. Faster and faster and faster she accelerated until her purple blur began to whip up a strong wind.

Running for cover, many of the soldiers were blown down by the hurricane-like wind. Several grabbed the chains to keep from being blown away. The jester was swept off his feet and would have been whisked out of the hall had it not been for his strings. Deliah held down her dress so as not to reveal Arabella.

Jackaranda had never been madder! The howling wind fused with her strange lament and resonated throughout the clock.

Outside, Albert, Horseradish, and Topp C. had crept back to the fire engine to wait for Flip-Flop.

Suddenly the clock started to shake and dust poured out of every crack and crevice. The wind inside grew stronger and stronger, hurling mountains of debris onto the ground.

Then to the utter astonishment of the trio, soldiers began to fly out of the main entrance. The chrome tricycle was the first, followed by the wooden cow on wheels. As the Jackarandan winds increased, more soldiers were catapulted out. Some attempted to cling to the doorway, but most lost their grip and were hurled into The Forest.

A loud screech came from the cuckoo's nest high atop the clock. The door to the bird's home snapped open and a flurry of feathers clouded the air. Out sprang the terrified bird, whose feet were glued to his sliding platform.

"Akkkk! What do you think this is, a windmill? Two more minutes and I'll be bald as a plucked chicken. Akkkk!"

"Deliah and Arabella!" Albert screamed. "I've got to go help them!"

Horseradish protested, "You can't go in there. Remember you are only a boy."

But Albert was gone. The boy tried to run to the clock's entrance, but gale winds forced him back. Again he tried, but he was blown down. Not one to give up, Albert got to his feet and pushed against the hurricane. He neared the large crack when a xylophone was hurled from the clock, colliding with him.

"Ouch!" cried the boy as he was blown to the edge of The Forest. Albert was hurt.

Recovering, he tried again—only to be bombarded with more debris. Once again the brave boy was pushed back into The Forest. Horseradish was there to meet him.

"Albert, it's useless," the red horse pleaded. "The winds are too strong."

"But Flip-Flop may need me," he cried. "I can't leave them alone." He arose once more to make another attempt.

"Ahhhh!" yelled a drum that flew into the boy halfway to the entrance.

Horseradish and Topp C. had seen enough. The top grabbed the cut and bruised boy, tossed him over Horseradish's saddle, and the horse galloped away. Albert passed out.

Inside the clock, Jackaranda continued to spin at lightning speed. Then suddenly the purple blur began to change color. Very subtly at first, then quite rapidly, the bright purple gave way to an unpleasant green.

No Name watched all this very calmly, but finally he had enough. He reeled the flying jester back in to him.

The frightened puppet yelled, "I'm warning you, Jackaranda, if you don't stop you shall never get your smile back."

Jackaranda began to slacken her speed. The threat worked. The wind stopped as the exhausted jack ceased her twirling. The dazed soldiers began to reassemble in front of the throne.

Jackaranda toppled over to rest on one of her four pointed arms. Dribble rolled out from behind the mainspring when he saw his mistress fall. Cautiously, he bounced close to her. "S-s-she's s-s-surely s-s-spun s-s-sickly green!" hissed the astonished ball.

All were shocked to see that Jackaranda had indeed changed color. No longer was she a shiny purple, but her metal had corroded and become a coarse and crusty green. Green with envy!

Dribble raced over to help her up, but she pushed him away. And with mindless bravura, she raved on, still out of breath. "What did you think of my performance, Great No Name? *Incredible*, no?"

"Subtle," replied the voice for the Master. "Very subtle."

As Jackaranda curtsied she saw that her standing point was no longer purple.

"*¿Qué pasa?* What's happening?" she screamed racing over to Windows, the cracked looking glass, cowering in the corner. She dragged the mirror, broken by some of the flying debris, to the center of the room and for the first time saw herself full length.

"Ye, aye, aye, aye!" she screamed. "*Verde*, I've turned *verde*! Green! Dribble, come polish me quick!"

Carrying a large rag, the ball bounced over and began to rub her corroded metal furiously.

"*¿Qué pasa?* What happened?" she demanded.

No Name stared as the jester said, "You coveted what was not yours, and in so doing, you lost that which you already had—your beauty!"

Startled and humiliated, she gazed once more at her reflection. Her ugliness caused Windows' glass to shatter even more. What she saw so repulsed her that she spun sobbing toward her private chamber in the clock. Dribble bounced obediently behind, prodding the unwilling Windows along with him.

"¡Rana! ¡Rana!" screamed the jack. "A frog! I look like a giant tree frog!" Her shrill voice echoed throughout the old clock as her spinning green blur disappeared.

CHAPTER NINETEEN

The Sideshow

RATTLES, WHO HAD BEEN holding Colette by her arms, released her and ordered the unsmiling flip-flop doll to clean up the mess that had been made by Jackaranda's hurricane.

Deliah swept some of the debris into a far corner as Arabella whispered, "Let's get out of here now! They'll never notice us in all this confusion."

"Shhhh," warned Deliah, "we must first find out where he keeps the smiles. It's Kriss Kringle's only hope."

"Oh, sawdust," mumbled Arabella. "Then we'll surely get broken now."

No Name left the throne room to think while the results from Jackaranda's outburst were cleaned away. As he departed, he hung his puppet's cross-sticks on a large hook near the throne. From that position the jester could observe all that was going on.

Colette glanced over at him. He didn't really seem to be interested in giving orders now, as he sat quietly with his head bowed. Colette walked over to him.

"Stay away from me," he snapped as he saw her approach. "I said stay away!"

But Colette was not frightened. She sensed a great sadness and vulnerability in the jester.

"Tell me, monsieur, why do you speak ze words for No Name? Can't he talk for himself?"

The jester did not answer, but continued to look down sadly.

Determined to have her questions answered, she tried a different tactic.

"I'll bet you were ze funniest puppet to ever come out of zis sack," flattered Colette.

He looked up at the ballerina, his eyes growing even sadder as he remembered his last journey out of Kriss's red sack.

"I'll bet all ze children laughed when you performed," coaxed Colette. "*Oui*? Am I not right, monsieur?"

The mournful puppet finally spoke. This time his voice didn't boom nor seem frightening. "Children used to come for miles to see my show. I was billed as 'Bellvedere and his Puppeteer.' The world's youngest and funniest puppet show."

"Please tell me more, monsieur. I want to know everything about you."

Slowly Bellvedere found the words. "Yes, I belonged to the world's youngest puppeteer and we travelled in the 'Greatest Travelling Circus in the World.' Theo, my puppeteer, was only nine years old, but already we had become very famous. We were not yet allowed to perform in the center ring, but we had a place of honor in the sideshow."

Colette, sensing Bellvedere would not object, sat down next to him.

"Theo was a one-year-old when his father bought me from a Gypsy wagon. We had a dream that one day we would play the center ring," he continued. "My friend and I practiced hard. Hour upon hour, day after day, we went over our routines until no one could watch us without laughing."

The memories pained him and his voice began to waver. "The laughter of the children was always my greatest reward."

"What brought you back here to ze great sack?"

"We were sharing a berth, travelling on a train to our next stop, when, during the rainy night, it must have jumped the track," he lamented. "The next thing I remember, I was rolling over and over and over. When the car came to a stop, I looked over at Theo and saw that he was not breathing. He had gone away . . . forever. It was only then that I realized how broken *I* was."

"*Terrible*," wept Colette. "You must have been very lonely."

But the jester had cried all that long-ago night and now he had no more tears to shed.

"I couldn't wait to get back inside the red sack. I knew that Handyman was waiting and that I would soon be repaired and sent to another happy home." The puppet bowed his head. "And I shall never forget my dear friend Theo. I hope he, too, has been repaired."

Wiping her eyes, the dancer sighed, "Zen how can you be so mean-tempered now? What makes you say such horrible things to ze others?"

"When I came through the kaleidoscope, instead of finding Handyman, I was captured and selected to be the voice of No Name. When he holds my strings, his intense anger and hatred flow from his hands, down the strings, and into my body. I can't help but be mean and nasty. I can sense what he wants me to say. So you see, I am completely under his control until he releases me," confessed the sorrowful puppet.

"But Monsieur Bellvedere, why don't you run away?"

Bellvedere looked around the clock at all the sad soldiers carrying out their various tasks. "We can't leave here. No Name has the key to our locked-away smiles and threatens never to release them unless we help him ruin Christmas. The thought of never smiling or being played with by a child again is more than we can bear. So we have to follow him. But there *is* one thing I can't figure out—why your smile has been spared."

This frightened Colette. The thought of losing her smile was unthinkable. She had to act quickly. "*S'il vous plaît*—please—won't you tell me," she cajoled, "where are ze locked-away smiles?"

Suddenly Bellvedere jumped to his feet. "He's coming; he's coming, now!"

Fanfare had just returned fully repaired, and commenced to trumpet. But instead of the beautiful sound he expected, out came the same loud off-key tooting as before. His shiny new luster couldn't change the sound of his sorrow.

Colette fled back to her corner and watched as No Name grabbed the jester's strings. For a moment she could see bright lightninglike sparks race from the Master's hands, down through the strings, and into Bellvedere.

"All hail, His Grace has arrived, you trash-bin recruits!" bellowed the volatile puppet, now, once again, under the leader's spell.

The soldiers, including Flip-Flop, immediately fell to their knees.

"I thought I told that trumpet to go to the workshop and get repaired," Bellvedere screamed.

"I did, Your Gracefulness. They hammered out my dents, polished up my brass, but what comes out is still not right. I can't seem to sound any pretty notes."

Bellvedere had no time to waste on this whining trumpet. "Then don't bother to trumpet again! You are hereby forbidden!"

Downcast, Fanfare accepted the decree and joined the other soldiers. Not only had his smile been removed, but now his very usefulness was stripped away.

No Name, that puzzling glaze still in his eyes, stared at Colette.

Bellvedere spoke for him. "There is still the matter of your becoming queen. It must be done at once."

"Let ze jack, Jackaranda, be queen and let me return to Ze Forest," pleaded Colette. "She obviously wants ze crown. Besides, Jackaranda and No Name would be a perfect match."

"The decision has been made!" snapped Bellvedere and the guards drew their swords. The discussion was over.

Colette stalled, "Well, if I am to stay, ze least you could do is have my music box brought to me. I cannot live without it. It contains everything I treasure. I couldn't possibly become your queen until it is returned to me."

No Name's glare softened a bit. A look of surprise crossed Colette's face as she became aware of the change. Could it be there was some kindness left inside this monster?

"It shall be done, but the moment your music box is retrieved, there will be no further delays," insisted the jester.

"*Merci beaucoup*, monsieur," sighed Colette, feigning gratitude.

She had stalled him. Maybe it would give her enough time to figure out an escape plan. If only that strange toy, Albert, were here. He was different somehow. He might be able to help.

"Oh, Monsieur Albert, where are you?" she pined.

CHAPTER TWENTY

The Flight

ALBERT AWOKE SCREAMING, "Arabella! Deliah! I must 'elp the flip-flop doll." He tried to move, but his badly injured body ached all over.

"Lie still," calmed Handyman and lifted his ten hands, as the warm gust reappeared. Gently, he laid all his hands on Albert and great waves of heat rippled throughout the boy's damaged body.

Moments later, Handyman stepped back and instructed him to sit up. Albert hesitated but the pain was gone and the cuts and bruises had disappeared. Albert was healed. The fixer of toys had repaired the boy!

Dazed, Albert got to his feet. "Oh, thank you, sir."

Handyman nodded and smiled. "I am told you were very brave."

"I 'ave just got to find another way inside that clock. Arabella and Deliah might be 'urt," Albert cried, now almost fully recovered.

"The strong winds have died down," reported Handyman. "There is no more we can do now except wait and see if the winds will start up again. That is, unless you have another plan."

Albert felt that the strange old creature was testing him. But the boy eagerly accepted the challenge. "I need to know everythin' about this 'ere place," he demanded. "'Andyman, you must please answer my questions."

The ten-handed creature nodded yes.

"First of all, 'ow do the toys get 'ere? I asked Colette, but she said this was 'er first time to the red sack and it was all so amazin' and things 'appened so quickly that she could not begin to explain it."

A calm born of great knowingness seemed to overtake the ancient creature and he moved over, indicating that the boy sit next to him. Once again that warm breeze encircled Handyman and caused his long blue whiskers to stir gently.

"Colette is a brand-new toy," he began. "When she was made she had no idea that we existed."

"But 'ow do all the toys make it 'ere over the enormous distances? There are toys in 'ere from places I never even dreamed about."

"After a toy is broken and realizes it is not to be repaired or played with again, something glorious happens while the world is sleeping. As I explained to you when I showed you the golden pouch, its smile has already travelled here to await the toy's arrival. Alone, without its smile, the toy's little red heart breaks and splits in two."

What he said touched deep down in Albert's heart, for he too felt his had broken when Tezzy died.

"The halves of the heart fly out of the lonely toy and circle in opposite directions around it. Around and around they soar, making certain it is truly time to return. When satisfied, they flutter down and alight on the toy's back, landing side by side. They ever so gently touch."

"Oh, please, sir, tell me more," begged Albert.

Handyman smiled, remembering the first time he had heard of this transformation. "Then a truly magical thing happens," he continued. "The two red halves begin to quiver and shake. Slowly both begin to unfurl and spread; growing larger and larger until they can stretch no more."

Albert's mouth gaped open wide as he listened to this incredible story.

"There, attached to the back of the abandoned toy, its heart has transformed itself into two large red wings."

A gasp was all the boy could manage.

"The beautiful gossamer wings flutter in the night's air, allowing the toy to forget his pain and loss."

"What 'appens next?" pleaded Albert.

"The wings lift the toy high above the earth where it engages a moonbeam to guide it here. At the end of the broken toy's journey, it glides into the mouth of the great sack and the majestic wings release the toy, allowing it to tumble down toward the kaleidoscope. The wings begin to shrink and fold, becoming once more the little broken heart. Gently, the two halves re-enter the toy and are immediately mended, once he is reunited with his smile. Now repaired, the toy awaits in happy anticipation the day he can return to the World of Play."

Albert sobbed, "Is that what will 'appen to me when I die? Will I 'ave Red Wings?"

Handyman reached out his ten arms and held the child close. "Albert, what happens when your time comes is a wondrous adventure, the crowning of a lifetime. As it was for Colette, let it be a surprise; and when you can no longer hold on to your world, enter the next with love and acceptance."

Albert began to ask another question, but stopped. Looking into Handyman's eyes he felt at peace. No more answers were needed.

CHAPTER TWENTY-ONE

The Spy

IT HAD CERTAINLY BEEN a day filled with surprises for the Army. The disheartened soldiers couldn't wait until Christmas Day had passed, for then they hoped that No Name would relent and give them back their smiles.

A sudden commotion erupted from the back of the hall as the smiling patchwork blue cat, who had earlier slipped quietly into The Forest, pushed his way toward the front.

How dare a smiling toy enter these premises! And how had he gotten in?

"Seize that cat!" Rattles commanded. "Take his smile!" The soldiers moved into action.

"Release him!" countered the jester. "Let him approach me—unharmed."

Now the Army was really confused. First, the ballerina, now the cat. Both their smiles were spared! Why?

The cat scampered to the jester and bowed.

"What took you so long, Swatches?" snarled the jester.

The cat attempted to respond but his voice was muffled and his words couldn't be understood.

"Oh, I forgot . . . your disguise. Take it off," Bellvedere directed.

The Army gasped as the cat reached up with his paw and slowly removed his painted cardboard smile. Hidden underneath was a nasty frown. His smile had been pasted on!

"Well, what *did* take you so long?" repeated the jester.

"I got lost, Your Highness," Swatches replied meekly.

"Well, you incompetent overstuffed mouser, what do you have to report?" snapped Bellvedere.

"There's a human in the sack. A little boy!" announced the patchwork cat.

No Name's eyes glowed like a raging fire. A child! There was nothing he hated more than a child.

"Impossible!" yelled Bellvedere. The leader turned his back on his troops to conceal his agitation and left his puppet to face them.

"It's true, I saw him in The Forest of Broken Parts," said a trembling Swatches.

The cat had to be mistaken! A boy in the great red sack was unthinkable. What next?

"But, Master," purred Swatches cautiously, "that's not all."

"Well, what is it? Speak up!"

The cat whispered into Bellvedere's ear and the jester's face began to contort.

"It seems the Pretty Ones have sent a spy to our clock," sneered the jester to the Army.

"A spy? Here amongst us? How could he have gotten in?" their whispers swelled.

"And I intend to weed him out," smirked the jester. "As for you, tatty tomcat, if you had stayed longer, you would know who the spy is. But now I'm forced to uncover the intruder in my own way."

The patchwork cat cowered back, knowing there was no escape.

Flip-Flop began to shake.

"The spy is probably here amongst us," Bellvedere continued. "And it's all your fault, Swatches. I make you responsible." Turning to Rattles he ordered, "Unstuff this cat!"

"No! Please don't! Not that!" the cat meowed.

But it was too late. A group of soldiers grabbed the blue cat and carried him yowling out of the Hall of Greatness. His loud cries continued as they dragged him from the clock.

Colette was terrified. Was this to be her fate also?

The jester turned his attention back to the soldiers. His evil and menacing look made Deliah frown even harder to maintain her disguise.

"Now we are in for it," whined Arabella from underneath. "I knew we'd be discovered!"

"Quiet!" whispered Deliah, slapping at her skirt. "As long as I frown we'll be safe."

"I shall now locate our uninvited guest. As you know, none of us in No Name's Army can laugh. Only the Pretty Ones can do that," Bellvedere reminded.

"My last time out of this great sack, I was the star puppet in a circus." Remembering his last days of glory, he took a long, low bow. "And I would now like to perform some of my favorite routines."

No Name lifted the marionette and placed his controls on the large hook to give Bellvedere more freedom to move. Once No Name released him, the sizzling sparks flew up the strings, past the wooden controls, through the air, and leapt back into No Name's hands. Once free, Bellvedere caught Colette's eyes and they exchanged a brief look. Then he began a series of acrobatic cartwheels and backflips, headstands to splits, pratfalls and silly dances.

Colette watched the sad little creature's performance and noticed something changing in his face. The more he performed, the more he became involved in his act until he seemed to forget that he was still in the cuckoo clock. Instead he was reliving his days in the sideshow with Theo and the laughing audiences.

The more he believed in his routines, the funnier they became. Even the flip-flop doll was getting caught up in his performance.

Colette had to smile. Deliah struggled to keep her frown while Arabella couldn't resist peeking.

The jester added jokes to his routine as Rattles marched menacingly up and down the ranks looking sternly at their faces. Just a trace of a smile would betray the spy.

Arabella almost giggled but Deliah quickly slapped her skirt to shut her up.

Colette could resist no longer. Bellvedere was just too funny. A giggle escaped her pretty mouth. No Name turned sharply to face her. The rage in his eyes silenced her. She put her hands over her mouth to stifle any further laughs.

No Name seized the puppet's strings.

"Silence! Or your smile will be removed and placed in the Chest of Smiles," cautioned the jester as the sparks reentered his body.

"The Chest of Smiles?" Colette's eyes pleaded for an answer.

The jester responded by moving to the throne and raising the blue velvet draping it. He revealed a massive golden box bound in heavy chains secured by a large lock. He kicked the box. To Colette's surprise, the sound of muffled laughter came from within.

"Any more out of you, dancer, and your smile will be put away in there and locked up forever."

No Name released the jester, allowing him to resume his act. As the sparks retreated up the strings Bellvedere looked at her pleadingly as if to say, "I've shown you where he keeps the smiles. Now, please help us."

He began to imitate animals, becoming more outrageously funny. For him, the grim faces of the soldiers became the smiling faces of the children. For the first time since that night on the train, he felt joy trying to mend his broken heart.

"Cluck, cluck, cluck," he mimicked, as he walked around with his hands under his arms flapping his elbows up and down. His conviction was infectious.

Despite her fear, Deliah had trouble holding in her laughter. This jester must have been very popular in the circus because he was the funniest thing she had seen in a long while. But with Rattles near, she *had* to keep quiet.

As Rattles passed Deliah, he heard muffled giggling.

"Did you say something, soldier?" he snapped.

"No, sir," she frowned.

"Good," he replied and moved on.

"Will you keep it down, Arabella! He almost caught us!" whispered Deliah when he was out of earshot.

"I'm sorry. It won't happen again," mumbled Arabella.

Deliah was glad that the jester was nearing the end of his act. It had been difficult, but they had made it. They hadn't been found out.

The sounds of the jester croaking like a frog and jumping around were too much for Arabella to ignore. She lifted her skirt and peeked.

Then Bellvedere caught her off guard. Turning around, without warning, he dropped his satin trousers to reveal brightly colored polka-dot shorts. As if that weren't enough, he pulled down the polka-dot shorts and uncovered still another pair. Painted on them was his own smiling face. Arabella could hold back no longer. This was too funny. She exploded into whoops of laughter.

"Seize her! Seize that laughing spy," Rattles ordered.

The flop-eared dog standing next to Deliah grabbed her arm but Arabella, from her upside-down position, grabbed one of his stuffed feet and tripped him. The surprised dog fell down and barked, "Look out, there are two of them!!"

Arabella and Deliah flip-flopped for their lives.

"Run! Run!" yelled Colette.

She looked over at Bellvedere and saw a tear had escaped his eye. He looked up at her sadly and whispered, "I'm sorry. I had to make them laugh."

The Army was closing in. They had spread out in many directions, blocking off all exits of escape for Arabella and Deliah, who quickly flip-flopped into a corner and were trapped—until Deliah spied the large chains that led to the cuckoo's home. She grabbed one of them and started to climb. Arabella looked down from her vantage point to see the Army approaching.

"Hurry, Deliah, hurry! They're gaining!"

The soldiers, too, began to scale the chains. Others were mounting the rickety wheels to get to them. Arabella resolved to do something! She grabbed one of the chains and shook it, causing the soldiers to lose their grip and fall.

"Quick thinking," cheered Deliah.

But now there were the soldiers on the gears to contend with. They were getting closer.

Deliah looked around in desperation. She noticed a light coming from above where the cuckoo lived.

"There," she yelled. "We've got to get up there. It's our only hope!"

"We'll never make it," Arabella cried. "The opening's too narrow."

Undaunted, Deliah snapped, "We have to. So you'll just have to blow out all your hot air and make yourself as thin as possible."

Both exhaled as hard as they could. Deliah stuck her head through the opening while Arabella pushed from underneath. The Army continued to close in. Huffing and puffing, they squeezed through the hole and found themselves in the cuckoo's perch. Success!

"Akkkk! Akkkk! So glad you could make it!" the bird shrieked in reaction to these intruders.

"He'll shred us to pieces!" screamed Arabella.

"Hush," warned Deliah as she turned to the bird. "Nice birdie. You're such a nice birdie," she soothed.

But the attempt didn't work. He was too angry. His eyes narrowed to slits. "Arrrk! Arrrk! Don't you 'nice birdie' me," he cried. "I needed a new mattress for my nest and you'll do just fine. Arrrk! Arrrk!"

The soldiers were almost within reach. Flip-Flop was caught between them and this violent black bird, who was screeching and pecking. The wind from his flapping wings whipped up thick clouds of dust that filled the air.

"Good-bye, old pal," sobbed Deliah.

"If only we could get out of this," cried Arabella, "I'd always let you have the upright position."

The bird was within inches of them, his sharp beak poised to tear them open. They closed their eyes to the inevitable. But a miracle happened. Both hands of the old timepiece collided at twelve o'clock, forcing the door of the roost to open and shoving the bird, whose feet were glued to the perch, outside to commence its twelve shrieks.

Cautiously, Arabella and Deliah opened their eyes to see that the door could provide them with a possible escape. They ran along the narrow wooden perch toward the bird. Now where?

"It's too far to jump," yelled Arabella.

Deliah looked back to see the Army had entered the nest and was on its way out to get them.

"Help! Help! Somebody help us!!"

The Army pressed on. If they weren't captured by the soldiers, the bird, having finished calling the hour, would be pulled back towards them and tear both to ribbons. Trapped!

But, no! Bright colors in the sky! Albert to the rescue! He appeared straddling Bree-Zing, the dragon kite.

"Over here," signaled Deliah. "We are over here."

Bree-Zing flew rapidly toward the cuckoo's perch as she and Albert spied the panicked Flip-Flop.

The bird shrieked, "Five." Only seven to go.

"Hurry, Albert, hurry!" cried Arabella just as one of the soldiers grabbed Deliah's red dress.

The kite came within inches of Flip-Flop. Albert reached down and caught hold of Deliah's two outstretched arms and Bree-Zing flew straight up. Flip-Flop was lifted slightly off the perch with the soldier clutching the red dress. Despite her mightiest efforts, the dragon kite couldn't spirit them away.

The bird shrieked its final "twelve." The old wooden perch jerked as it began slowly to pull the bird toward Flip-Flop.

"Oh, no," cried Arabella. Then another of the soldiers grabbed her dress. The screeching bird, now within reach, began pecking at them. Its sharp beak tore into the red material. In another moment, the door to the cuckoo's nest would slam shut and it would be the end of Flip-Flop.

With Bree-Zing trying to fly away and the soldiers clutching onto the dress, the strain was too great. A piece of the dress was torn completely off allowing the kite to pull Albert and the flip-flop doll up and away from the clock.

"What took you so long, honey?" scolded Deliah.

"No wind," joked Albert.

Deliah held tightly as they sailed to freedom.

"Akkkk! Akkkk! Don't leave! The party was just getting started!" squawked the bird as he watched the trio fly off. Then he began an all-out attack on the two soldiers holding the torn piece of red dress. They scrambled to get down the chains, causing the other soldiers to fall all over each other as they tried to avoid the beast's sharp beak.

Their cries became fainter and fainter as Albert and his friends flew jubilantly farther and farther away.

CHAPTER TWENTY-TWO

The Pond

FLYING HIGH ABOVE THE FOREST and the old clock, Albert took time to say, "Thank you, Bree-Zing. Good work."

"Think nothing of it," smiled the Chinese kite. "It's nice to have you travelling with me. It's always more fun when I have little sailors aboard."

"Little sailors," thought Albert, remembering his "queen." The outside world seemed so far away and that cold London night under the bridge was just a distant memory.

Bree-Zing negotiated a bank to the left, bringing Albert out of his daydream. He turned his attention to Deliah, who had grabbed hold of the dragon kite's tail.

Arabella, flying upside down, pleaded, "Please Deliah, let me hold onto Bree-Zing. I can't stand looking down."

Albert extended his hand. "Grab 'old of me, Arabella. That way you both can 'ang on to something."

The blonde doll gratefully accepted Albert's hand.

When they were all settled, Albert began, "Colette? Is she all right?"

"She's fine," replied Arabella, catching her breath. "But the strangest thing happened."

"I know," interjected the boy. "I saw the wind blow the soldiers right out of the clock. It was very strange."

"Oh, that was Jackaranda throwing a hissy-fit," replied Arabella.

"It was stranger than that," Deliah, now facing the rear, yelled over her shoulder.

"What was it? What 'appened?"

"Nothing."

"Nothing? But why is that so strange?"

"No Name let Colette keep her smile!" piped Arabella, beating Deliah to the punch.

"That *is* unusual," pondered Albert. "But were you able to find out where 'e keeps the other smiles?"

"Yes," Deliah answered proudly. "He sits on them! He uses the golden chest for his throne! But the Chest of Smiles is locked up tight, and we couldn't find where he keeps the key."

Albert was pleased with this piece of information and smiled, "Good work, ladies."

Then he turned to look at the land below. From this height he could see the limitless horizon and all its wonder. The sky had a rosy cast. Handyman's abandoned workshop looked forlorn deep in The Forest of Broken Parts. Suddenly, something shiny and sparkling in the distance caught his eye.

"Bree-Zing, please fly us over there."

"Aye, aye, captain," the kite responded obligingly.

"Oh, Albert," pleaded Arabella, "aren't we going to land soon? I don't think I can hold on much longer."

"Try, Arabella. Albert must have a reason for taking this detour," assured Deliah.

Bree-Zing's wonderfully colored serpentine body floated toward the object of Albert's curiosity. As they drew nearer, she recognized the landmark and exclaimed, "Why that's The Pond—The Pond of I-Wish-I-Were."

"That's where the Grablies were going to become tin soldiers," added Arabella.

This was the third time Albert had heard The Pond mentioned. What was it?

Bree-Zing flew directly above The Pond. Below, a vast array of No Name's troops were lined up single-file in front of the small round pool.

Un-Bear-Able was standing at the edge staring at his reflection in what appeared to be a mirror. The surface of The Pond lay so still, his reflection was crystal-clear. Then he began talking to himself. Almost imperceptibly at first and then quite rapidly, his reflection began to change into that of a tin soldier.

When his new image was complete and as clear as the old one had been, the bear dived into The Pond and disappeared. The ripples he made in the strange liquid did not radiate away from where he had entered The Pond, but rather came towards the spot. Reappearing seconds later, he was no longer a Teddy bear. He had transformed into a tin soldier.

Albert was speechless.

Each Grablie took his turn at The Pond's edge, transforming himself into a tin soldier. Though not identical in costume or nationality, they all became metal soldiers.

"Bree-Zing, I've seen enough. Please fly us back to camp as quickly as you can," Albert implored.

Bree-Zing veered starboard.

As the kite soared into view, a joyous cry erupted from the Pretty Ones who had been waiting anxiously. Arabella and Deliah were safe and now they would have news.

Bree-Zing landed her passengers in her usual way—by collapsing. Albert and Flip-Flop somersaulted over and over across the ground. As they recovered, the other toys gathered around them.

"Colette's all right for now," Albert explained, "and Flip-Flop 'as located the Chest of Smiles."

The toys cheered.

"That's all I can tell you. Best let Arabella and Deliah describe what 'appened inside the clock."

Arabella and Deliah began telling of their detective work. Arabella, as always, was being quite dramatic. She just loved hearing herself talk and knew that others did, too.

Her discourse reached its high point when she told of the incident of the black and red cuckoo bird's attack. "If he had come any closer, I would have plucked every feather off that overgrown chicken!"

Samson strode over to Arabella and gave her a small kiss. "You are soooo brave, Arabella."

"Yes, I know," she swooned, playing the heroine.

"Flip!

"Aren't you forgetting something, dear Arabella?" teased Deliah, now on top. "Since we have made it back home safely, I get to always be in the upright position."

"Oh, sawdust," sighed Arabella, remembering her promise back at the clock. Deliah chuckled.

"What about our sister, Jackaranda?" Flap Jack asked.

"She better not be hurt," threatened Jack Knife.

"She's there all right and she is not hurt, only . . ." Deliah stopped, not wanting to say any more.

"Go on and finish," insisted Jack-Of-All-Trades.

Arabella poked her head out through the tear in the red dress and blurted, "She has become so jealous of Colette that her purple metal turned green with envy."

"Green!" the nine jack brothers echoed in astonishment. They felt very sad upon hearing the news.

"We warned you, she's always had a bad temper," cowered Jackal, "but we love her, just like all the children did."

"She was always quite a lady, very refined," Jack-a-Dandy added.

"She must be scared," trembled Jack-O'-Lantern.

"I'll give you money they've done something mean to her," bet Black Jack.

"Hurry! Hurry! Hurry!" sobbed Jack Rabbit. "Let's jump to it. Hippity-hop. Hippity-hop."

Jack-A-Roo reminded, "Well, mates, with her missing, a little girl can only go through her onesies to ninesies. We need Jackaranda to get to tensies."

"Oh, Albert," they all cried, "what can we do?"

Turning around, they discovered he had disappeared, for Albert needed to talk to Handyman and he hadn't wanted the others to overhear.

Handyman was standing alone with his eyes closed and his ten hands clasped together when the boy interrupted.

"'Andyman, I saw something unusual out there. It is somethin' you forgot to explain."

Opening his eyes, Handyman listened to the events at The Pond before taking a seat on a broken wheel.

"Alas, I fear we have reached the end," he mumbled to himself.

"What's 'appening?" asked Albert. "Is it bad?"

"I'm afraid so," Handyman sighed. "Every one hundred years, a toy has the option of changing into another toy if he so desires. It can be anything it wants. A doll who is tired of being a doll can choose to become a ball or a top. It merely has to wish for it at The Pond."

"Now I am really confused," Albert moaned as he sat down near Handyman. "'Ow does all that work?"

Handyman showed signs of impatience, got up, and began to pace. That familiar warm breeze reappeared.

"A toy which has not used The Pond in at least a century merely looks at its own reflection. Then it repeats, 'I wish I were; I wish I were,' over and over as it visualizes the toy it wishes to become. If its concentration is strong enough, and its commitment firm, its reflection will mirror that which it wishes to be."

"Oh, I get it! Then the toy dives into The Pond and grabs 'old of its new reflection," Albert deduced.

"Exactly," confirmed Handyman. "When the toy resurfaces, it has become that which it wished to be."

"But why would No Name send 'is Grablies to The Pond to become tin soldiers?"

"To become fighters!" explained Handyman sadly. "It will now be much easier to capture us all."

They were now surrounded by the other toys who had come to find Albert. Handyman's last words had been heard by all.

"Oh, no, Handyman! What are we going to do?" cried the frightened toys. "What *are* we going to do?!"

CHAPTER TWENTY-THREE

The Trojan Horse

MOLLY, THE RAG DOLL, ran to Horseradish for comfort. Others began shaking and clutched each other tightly, fearing the day they would be broken by the Grablies.

"I haven't any solutions and time is running out," confessed Handyman.

"If only we knew 'is weakness," pondered Albert.

"His weakness . . ." Handyman repeated slowly to himself. Then his eyes sparkled and a smile crossed his face. "Maybe . . . just maybe!"

"Please, tell us what is it that's on your mind.
"The answer to the question did you find?"

Topp C. quizzed.

As the blue-haired creature turned and looked to the boy, the warm gust of wind blew gently into Albert's face.

"'Is smile!" Albert suddenly piped in. Handyman nodded in approval. "If he 'ad his smile back, he would 'ave to change his ways!"

"The power of a smile is unbeatable," confirmed Handyman.

"But his smile won't stick," reminded Horseradish. "You told us that already." The other toys sadly agreed.

Handyman opened his jacket and retrieved the golden pouch from his hidden pocket. "Albert, I have no weapons to give you, for we are creatures of peace."

Albert remembered what Topp C., Horseradish, and Flip-Flop had said earlier, how Handyman felt about using weapons to hurt.

"But maybe," confessed Handyman as he handed the boy the golden pouch, "just maybe, if you can catch No Name with his guard down, release his smile. It's possible he will be unable to stop it from sticking."

"I'll give it me best," replied an unconvinced Albert, but he accepted the pouch and placed it gently in his pocket.

A small giggle was audible from within.

❄

"One more thing, please," Albert begged. "Me old clothes. Can I have 'em back please, sir? I can't move about as easily in these fancy rags."

Handyman snapped his fingers on all ten hands.

"I thought you might be wanting them."

Topp C. appeared shortly carrying Albert's old clothes. Holding out the tattered garments as if he didn't want to touch the unfashionable material, he said,

"It seems this drab and dreary cloth,
"Has been visited by a moth."

"Oh, thank you," sighed Albert and gratefully snatched the clothes from Topp C. It would be good to have something familiar around him once more. These brightly colored clothes made him feel ridiculous.

Albert dashed behind the broken locomotive chassis to change.

Out of sight, Albert hollered to Flip-Flop, "Did you say that they were going to fetch Colette's music box?"

"Yes, but why?" Deliah asked.

"We have to get back into that clock," Albert stated.

Arabella complained, "There's no way. They'll check everyone who goes in now. And most of them will be tin soldiers; so we're sure to stand out."

"You're right, Arabella," agreed Albert. "But if they don't know we are going in, they can't check."

Handyman asked the question on everyone's mind, "What are you talking about, boy?"

"Colette's music box!" he exclaimed. "We'll 'ide inside and let the soldiers carry us in."

"My dear ole chap, I do tip my cap.
"For this splendid idea, I do clap.

"With this strategy you'll need no force,
"Just like the Greeks and their Trojan horse.

"For the Greeks it did succeed indeed,
"Hiding soldiers in a hollow steed,"

rhymed Topp C., while the other toys whizzed and clanged their approval.

"I can't go back in there," protested Arabella, still under the folds of the red skirt.

Samson had been standing away from the others, but now moved purposefully over to Flip-Flop.

"And I thought you were brave, Arabella. I want my kiss back."

Arabella poked her head out and looked up at the iron boxer, knowing she had to restore herself in his eyes.

"I, uh . . . um," faltered Arabella, trying to think of a quick excuse to cover up her cowardice.

"She can't go," interrupted Albert, emerging from behind the train, now dressed in his own clothing. "I 'ave a more important job for you, Arabella."

She smiled with relief. She had been saved from embarrassment.

Samson saw her in a new light. She was important to the mission. He stepped forward and blew her another kiss.

"That's for good luck, peaches."

Arabella blushed and looked toward Albert. He gave her a quick wink and Arabella returned the same as if saying, "Thanks for covering for me."

Horseradish trotted to Albert and volunteered, "I want to go with you. Remember, I said I owed you one."

"Thank you, 'orseradish," and he hugged his friend. "I'm going to need someone to get Colette out of there in a 'urry if we get the chance. And you're just the one."

Topp C. spun closer.

> "What about me. Now don't forget.
> "I too want to help dear Colette."

"I could never forget about you, Topp C.," smiled Albert. "You are the fastest; so I want you to 'ide near the clock. When Colette's music box plays, spin back 'ere as fast as you can. You and Flip-Flop lead the others to the outside of the old clock."

> "Flip-Flop will do it winningly,
> "But I will do it spinningly."

Arabella, hearing that she didn't have to reenter the clock, feigned bravery. "Oh, fiddly bob. Is that *all* I get to do?"

The nine jacks spun to the front. Flap Jack spoke for his brothers. "There must be something we can do, too, pardner. We ain't goin' to sit on a rail while those hombres have got our purple sister."

"I 'ave a very special task for you lads," said the boy. "You must protect the others. Keep the Grablies out of reach."

Jack Knife stepped forward. "Nobody's gonna take my friends' smiles. I'll see to that."

The toys cheered.

Albert raised his voice so he could be heard above the commotion. "I want all you toys to follow Flip-Flop and start laughin'. Then run back into The Forest. That should anger those nasty Grablies enough to make 'em leave the clock and chase you. Then I'll be alone with No Name. You jacks will spin and form a line to protect the slower toys. But be very careful. Now that the Army is fixed and filled with tin soldiers, they are much more dangerous."

"Don't worry," said the multicolored jack, "we all know our jobs."

The meek Jackal stepped forward. "Even I will go. There are times like you said when you must protect your loved ones."

Hearing this, the entire toy population let out three cheers, led by Black Jack.

"Hip hip hurrah—hip hip hurrah—hip hip hurrah."

"What are you going to do to No Name, my brave boy?" inquired Handyman.

"I don't know for sure, sir. I'll just 'ave to take it as it comes. Now we must make it to the music box quickly, before the soldiers do!"

Just as he and Horseradish started to leave, the whole Forest swayed, causing many of the toys to lose their balance and fall.

"Oh, no!" cried Handyman.

"What is it?" screamed Albert.

"Shhhh," quieted the gentle creature.

Everyone fell silent, listening. Many tense moments passed until . . . the sound of jingle bells filled the air.

"It must be Christmas Eve! Kriss Kringle is loading his sleigh to begin his night's journey; the new toys will be arriving soon," moaned Handyman.

The toys groaned and sighed, wondering if there would be enough of them ready when Kriss reached into the sack.

"We have so little time," stated Handyman. "We must stop the Grablies before they break us and all the new toys, too."

"Then we must 'urry," declared Albert and he motioned for Horseradish to follow him.

"Good luck," encouraged the toys as they headed into The Forest.

"Pick up your feet and don't trip," reminded Handyman.

For a moment, Albert thought he had heard Mr. Lacy's voice calling after him. But that was crazy! Mr. Lacy was back in London in his toy shop, not in this sack!

Albert and Horseradish disappeared from the glen.

CHAPTER TWENTY-FOUR

A Time to Go

ALBERT AND HORSERADISH RACED toward the dingle, where the music box sat.

"Shhhh," warned Albert, "we 'ave to be careful."

Slowing down, they cautiously made their way through the scattered parts of The Forest until they saw the red-jeweled music box with its lid open. They were in luck. They had gotten there before the soldiers carried it off!

"Follow me!" whispered Albert.

He and Horseradish dashed to the music box and jumped inside. To their astonishment, they found the box filled with many elegant costumes, shining jewels, and even wigs!

"These might come in 'andy," commented Albert as he rummaged through the vast array of clothing.

"'Orseradish, what do you do 'ere when you are not fixing toys?"

"Oh, we have a grand time. For after the work is done, we all sit in a large circle and tell each other 'Children Tales'—stories about the humans we have known."

Albert thought of the stories Tezzy used to tell him each night before bed. Those wonderful fairy tales! But now they were real and his life outside the sack was the fantasy.

"Colette was lucky to have been out in the human world so long," sighed Horseradish, continuing to examine the ballerina's possessions.

Albert, detecting sadness in Horseradish's voice, turned from his rummaging. "Do you miss being out there?"

"Oh, yes," beamed Horseradish. "It's the most wonderful place. When someone loves you and plays with you, it's the best ever. I always feel so sad when I get broken and it's time to come back to the great red sack."

"'Ow long was your longest time out? " asked Albert.

"Eighty-seven years," reflected Horseradish. "I was a brightly colored rocking horse with a long silver tail. It was so much fun."

133

❄

"What 'appened?" inquired the boy.

Horseradish smiled. "Kriss Kringle gave me to a family named Costichek in Poland. They had a wonderful son, Orlov, who used to ride me for hours, laughing and dreaming of far-off places and adventures. Then he grew older and his interests changed. When his sister was born, I was handed down to her. She used to rock me every day. And groomed me after each ride. I loved them so."

"But they couldn't have played with you all those years. They 'ad to grow up."

"Everytime one grew too old for me, I was given to the next child. And then when Orlov was married, I went with him to his new home. There his children—and his grandchildren—and even his great-grandchildren—rode and loved me. They were so much like him."

"What 'appened to make you come back 'ere?"

"Oh, after years of playing and loving and galloping all those children to fanciful adventures, my wood became brittle. One day, I broke from over-use. Orlov's great-granddaughter was in the saddle and tumbled off onto the floor."

"Was she 'urt?"

"No," Horseradish smiled remembering. "Just a little frightened."

"So what 'appened?"

Horseradish saddened. "They tried to repair me, but I was too old. I had had too much use. My time was over. Orlov told the great-grandchildren that I wasn't safe, so they were forbidden to ride me anymore."

"You must 'ave been very sad," sympathized Albert.

Horseradish turned his face to hide the tears. "Orlov, now a very old man, carried me to the attic for storage. He put me in a dusty corner and started to close the door behind him, but then he stopped and stared at me for a long while. He slowly walked back over to me and ran his hand across my straggly mane one last time and started to cry.

"I can remember what he said as if it were yesterday. 'Good-bye, my favorite friend. Riding upon your back I have seen the world in my dreams. So, too, have my children and their children's children. You have been a trusted friend to us all, and shall be missed.'

"As tears fell, he quickly went to the door and closed it behind him. He never looked back. I knew it was time to sprout my wings for my journey back to this sack. Now Handyman has repaired me for someone new to love."

Tears welling, Albert remembered his loss of Tezzy.

"Almost every day I dream of my special families," Horseradish mused.

Suddenly, the sound of soldiers' footsteps broke their thoughts. Albert realized the lid to the music box was still opened. He motioned to Horseradish to help him close it lest they be discovered.

Four of No Name's new tin soldiers entered the dingle carrying two large wooden poles. They were led by an Irish whirligig, wearing a green vest and carrying a walking stick. As he marched, the wind caused his two arms to spin. The four soldiers laid the poles down so they were parallel. Then they went over to the music box, lifted it, and placed it centered on the two poles. Each then took an end of the poles and hoisted it up.

"Hurry up, laddies," snarled Whirly McGigg, the whirligig. "Let's get this back to the clock. No Name is acting strangely, he is. You never know what blarney he might do if we tarry too long."

One of the soldiers challenged, "He had better take that dancer's smile or I'll . . ."

"Or you'll what?!" boomed Whirly McGigg.

When the soldier made no response, Whirly McGigg threatened, "You hold your tongue, laddie, or I'll break you myself till you are the size of a leprechaun."

The insubordinate soldier was silenced.

"All right, to the clock! March!"

They headed back into The Forest with Albert and Horseradish silently being jostled inside the music box.

When they reached the entrance to the clock, they were stopped by a Japanese samurai.

"Stop! Who goes there?" he challenged holding a long curved sword with both hands.

Whirly McGigg, with a motion of his spinning hands, halted his men. "We are under Commander Rattles' orders to retrieve the dancer's music box."

"First, I must inspect it," announced the samurai. "We want no more spies, so step aside."

From inside, Horseradish and Albert could hear the orders. Terrified, they buried themselves under a pile of Colette's dresses.

The four tin soldiers set the music box down and, following the Samurai's orders, they opened the lid. Looking inside carefully, he saw nothing, but poked his long sword into the pile of clothes twice just to be sure.

Albert and Horseradish were in luck. The blade did not find them out.

Satisfied there were no spies inside, the samurai lowered his sword and bowed. "Entrance is granted."

The soldiers closed the mirrored lid and lifted the music box again by the poles. They entered the old clock.

"That was close!" trembled Horseradish. "We almost got it."

"If you think *we* almost got it," whispered Albert, "wait 'til Colette sees the 'oles that soldier put in 'er dresses. I wouldn't want to be 'im!"

They both laughed nervously.

CHAPTER TWENTY-FIVE

The Out-of-Step Dancer

THE MUSIC BOX WAS CARRIED through the eerie black of the inner chambers. The booming voice of the jester chastising the Army for allowing Flip-Flop to escape resounded throughout the clock.

Inside her private chamber, Jackaranda was being polished by her servant Dribble. Her small, dusty room was lit by a solitary shaft of light struggling through a crack in the wall. The ball had been successful at restoring her lovely purple luster.

In the ray of light she twirled and admired her reflection in the mirror. "There, I am back to my beautiful purple self."

"S-s-she s-s-sure s-s-sparkles s-s-spectacularly," Dribble said to Windows. But the cracked mirror didn't answer for fear he might upset her and be totally shattered.

Satisfied, Jackaranda dismissed Windows and began to pace.

"I must be crowned queen. Life as a common soldier would be unthinkable."

"S-s-sure s-s-sounds s-s-sensible, s-s-señorita," hissed the slow-leaking ball.

"*Ay caramba.* I hate that little girl that left my brothers and me on the street to be run over by her father's carriage. I could still be playing 'Eggs-in-the-Basket.' I am beginning to hate children more and more."

"S-s-surely s-s-sad s-s-she s-s-seems," thought the ball.

"Dribble, I *must* make him take that ballerina's smile," her voice rose in anger. "Have you seen the way he looks at her?"

"Yes-s-s. S-s-surely, s-s-seems s-s-strange."

"If you will help me, I will see to it that you are duly rewarded. If not, you shall be duly deflated!"

Her shiny purple metal was starting to dull again as jealousy entered her thoughts. "I'll do anything to make sure I'm queen," she snarled. "Anything!"

Inside the throne room the soldiers arrived with Colette's music box and she immediately ran to it. She was greatly relieved to have it back.

"Messieurs, *s'il vous plaît*—please, be careful with zat," she gasped when the soldiers dropped it. She opened the lid gingerly, hoping all was in good order. But what she saw almost made her scream.

"Shhhh! Only whisper and listen," Albert cautioned before she could yell. "We are going to whisk you out of here."

"Oh, Monsieur Albert, I am so delighted to see you, but zis place is *filled* with soldiers. How can you get me out?"

Colette nervously looked around the Hall of Greatness and noticed No Name glance up at her. She nodded and turned back to her music box, pretending to be busy arranging her belongings.

"Colette, you must get No Name to ask you to dance," Albert instructed. "Tell 'im you want to change your costume as a surprise. Then come inside 'ere to dress."

"*Pourquoi?*" she asked. "Why?"

"Don't ask questions. Just do it. We don't 'ave much time," Albert insisted. "It's Christmas Eve."

"I know," she responded sadly. "I heard ze bells."

Colette closed the lid and walked determinedly to No Name. But Bellvedere stopped her.

"Zis isn't going to be easy," she thought.

"Listen, *ma petite* puppet," she said with new-found bravery, "would you ask your puppeteer if he would like me to dance for him?"

No Name turned to stare at her.

"No Name says 'no,'" Bellvedere answered.

"Tell your Master zat I just want to thank him for returning my music box." She stared into No Name's shadowy hood. "I want to repay him for his kindness."

There was a long pause as No Name returned her stare.

"No!" the jester finally stated.

Getting a little annoyed, Colette said sweetly, "Tell your Master zat I will promise not to laugh anymore if he lets me dance."

Again, another long pause.

"The bells have sounded. He has no time for your amusement. The answer is *still* no."

"*Très bien*," said Colette, even more frustrated. "Tell him I just want to celebrate my coronation by dancing for my king."

Colette began to pout, a way which had always worked to her advantage in the past. But not this time. After another long pause, the answer was still no.

"All right then," she angrily declared, "I'll just scream until he concedes!"

She fell into a temper tantrum, screaming at the top of her voice. She ran over to her music box and started banging on it. She picked up pieces of the clock and hurled them at the jester, creating a racket.

No Name did not want a repeat of the trouble caused by the earlier Jackarandan winds.

"All right!" yelled the jester as he ducked the flying objects. "But make it quick!"

Colette regained her composure and cooed in her sweetest voice, "*Merci.* It would be an honor. But first monsieur . . . I'll just slip into something a little more special." She turned and walked to the music box.

Rattles stopped her, "Where are you going?"

"Can't a lady have some privacy?" She stepped inside and slammed the lid behind her.

"Did you 'ave to bang so 'ard on the outside? I thought I would go deaf!" Albert whispered.

"I rather liked my performance," she responded sweetly.

Just then, a loud rumble reverberated throughout the hall.

The newly transformed Army led by Un-Bear-Able had returned.

"Halt!" ordered the new tin soldier. "Our transformations are complete, sir."

The great number of tin soldiers was an ominous sight. Their shiny metal looked as cold as their hearts.

"Very well done," admired Bellvedere as his master gazed proudly on his new troops. "No Name is pleased. Very pleased. Now there is no way those happy toys can escape us."

A loud cheer rang out from the Army, echoing throughout the old clock.

Jackaranda and Dribble reentered the throne room when they heard the commotion.

"Now," continued the jester. "Where is that bothersome ballerina?"

Rattles marched over to the music box and rapped.

"All right! Hurry up!" he demanded.

"Coming," she called from inside. "Stand back."

The lid to the music box flew open. The soldiers stared as the dancer emerged dressed in flowing, multicolored chiffon sewn with tiny silver bells. On her head was a blonde wig, slightly askew, and her face was hidden by a veil.

"*Mira*—look at her," whispered Jackaranda to Dribble. "She looks terrible! No Name will certainly choose me over her." But again the pangs of jealousy caused her already-dulled purple metal to begin changing color.

The dancer took her place on top of the music box in front of the mirrored lid and signaled for someone to turn the handle. Un-Bear-Able stepped from the ranks to obey and the music began. But her dance was very clumsy, not like the grace and beauty of her performance in The Forest.

The unusual melody seemed to annoy No Name. The dance continued, getting worse and worse with each movement. When she lost her footing and tripped over her long dress, the soldiers began to boo. It was an awful presentation, accented by the tinkling of the little silver bells.

Jackaranda saw her chance and immediately spun next to the clumsy dancer. "*¡Ay caramba!* So this is to be your queen," she scoffed. "She looks and dances more like a broken soldier."

The Army was in agreement and cheered the once-purple jack on.

"Let me show you how a queen should move," Jackaranda said as she spun gracefully around the dancer. It was to be a battle of the dance!

"Let the best dancer be queen," challenged Jackaranda. The troops cheered encouragement at the idea of a contest. But No Name did not seem to hear her. He was distracted.

"How dare No Name ignore me," thought Jackaranda, now beginning to glow green.

The dancer resumed her dance, if one could call it that. For every time she would try to turn or move, her feet caught in her dress.

No Name stared at the dancer, not seeing her dance at all. His eyes glowed as he reacted violently, not to her, but the music. The melody tormented him.

The dancer came off the music box and moved closer to No Name. Her movements were getting even more out of step.

"Tell the lassie to stop," pleaded Whirly McGigg, voicing the thought of the astonished gathering.

Bellvedere said nothing. No Name could not hear. He only stared at the music box, more tormented than ever. The pain had overwhelmed him.

Unaware of his distress, the booing soldiers only served to spur Jackaranda on. Now completely corroded green with envy, the jack spun gracefully around the room, her movements quite elegant.

The dancer moved closer and closer to No Name until Rattles felt she was getting too near. He drew his sword to stop her. But the awkward dancer pretended this was part of her dance and sashayed over, whereupon she took the shining sword from him with little resistance.

Rattles was stunned. Quickly she spun away, raising the sword over her head.

Now the soldiers cheered for the dancer.

Jackaranda hated to be upstaged, so she, too, grabbed a sword and began to imitate her competitor's dance.

Faster and faster spun the dancer. To the fascination of the soldiers, the little bells on her costume jangled loudly.

"Please cut my strings," yelled Bellvedere. "Free me, please." His cries went unnoticed by his master.

Furious at having lost the attention, Jackaranda threw down her sword and lunged for the one the dancer held. But the dancer, turning as fast as she could, released the saber, causing a high-pitched shrill as it rapidly cut through the air toward its target—the jester. Jackaranda, now off-balance, tried to grab onto the dancer, but instead she caught hold of the dancer's hair and veil. As she fell, off they came. To everyone's surprise there stood the smiling . . . Albert!

No Name saw nothing. The haunting melody had bewitched him.

The jester saw the sword coming directly toward him. He ducked down to pull his strings taut so they could be cut easily. "Oh, yes, please set me free!"

No Name did not move.

The soldiers were helpless. They watched the sharp blade twirl and spin like a buzz saw through the air. Great flashes of sparks crackled and blazed when the blade severed the puppet's strings, causing him to fall into a heap on the ground.

"Thank you!" he exclaimed. "Thank you!"

"Stop!" whimpered a strange, frightened voice. It was No Name's. No longer did he have the jester to act as his voice. "Stop that music! I can't stand it!" the frail voice repeated. "Please . . . stop. . . ."

CHAPTER TWENTY-SIX

The Wayward Glow

SUDDENLY FROM OUTSIDE the clock came the sounds of laughter. Great guffaws and chortles filled the air. The Pretty Ones, having been called by Topp C. at the first sounds of the music box, gathered just as Albert had requested. The toys had come en masse.

Arabella and Deliah were leading, standing on top of Chug the train, which was carrying many laughing toys. Panda and Molly were riding in a cart pulled by Samson. Chutney plodded along with a dozen others riding on his mirrored saddle. Every happy toy in the great red sack had come to help. Their laughing and singing sounded throughout the clock.

"Capture those toys!" voiced No Name, having regained some of his composure.

The Army turned on his orders and raced from the hall. Even the soldier cranking the handle on the music box stopped and joined the pursuit. The old clock rumbled as the charging Army ran, bounced, hopped, rolled, and spun together, led by the new tin soldiers.

The happy toys spied the first of No Name's army emerging from the clock and retreated to the safety of The Forest. Deliah ordered Chug to turn around and it chuggedy-chugged away as fast as it could.

The nine jacks spun briskly in the rear, between the advancing Army and retreating laughing toys. Forming an impenetrable barrier of glistening metal, with each of their four arms twirling, the jacks quickly knocked down the oncoming soldiers when they ventured too close. A Grablie was about to capture one of the baby dolls when Jackal broke formation and fearlessly spun to her rescue. Quickly, the soldier was toppled.

A wedge of soldiers attacked from the side, but Samson rolled his barbells in their direction.

"Strike!" he yelled, as they were bowled over like bowling pins.

The slower toys now put more distance between the Grablies and themselves.

Horseradish, observing that most of the soldiers had exited the hall, leaped out of the music box with Colette riding in his saddle. In a great burst of energy, he galloped away, through the few stragglers, toward one of the large cracks—and freedom!

Startled, Rattles grabbed Albert and yelled, "Get those two!" But Albert managed to break free and run.

Jackaranda sneered, "¡*Ahora!* Now, Dribble, do your stuff." The rainbow ball began bouncing up and down, up and down, then rolled toward the fleeing boy.

Horseradish and Colette almost reached the opening but suddenly encountered a small group of tin soldiers coming from another part of the clock. Trapped! Colette jumped off the red horse and ran. But a few steps farther she was captured.

"I'm sorry, Colette," whinnied Horseradish. "I ran as fast as I could."

"It was a valiant effort," the ballerina responded as she was dragged, kicking, toward the Hall of Greatness.

Struggling, Horseradish and Colette were brought before No Name. Now that the music had ceased, his look of pain and anguish was replaced by that of confusion.

Albert neared the entrance. He would be free. But Dribble caught up with him and rolled between his feet, causing the boy to tumble to the ground. Rattles, close behind, snared the fallen boy and began to drag him back to the throne.

"Good work, Dribble," congratulated Jackaranda as the ball bounced back to her side.

"S-s-shucks, s-s-simple s-s-strategy," accepted the proud Dribble.

"If you are Colette, then who are you?" bellowed No Name as he looked from the ballerina to Albert. "And what toy are you?"

"'Ere we go again," thought the boy.

"I'm Albert!" he answered, breaking away from his captor. "And I ain't no toy! I'm a boy!"

"So," snapped No Name somewhat dumbfounded, "you are the boy we heard about. The one who's ruined my day. You'll pay for interfering with my plans!"

"Oh, yeah?" volleyed Albert as he ran to the music box, closed the lid, and jumped on top.

"Yes!" countered No Name. "Bring the dancer and the horse to me! He'll see what happens to intruders!"

The soldiers dragged them closer to the throne.

"Take the horse's smile!" commanded No Name.

"No!" pleaded Albert. "Leave 'im alone!"

Horseradish tried to bolt free but his reins were held too tightly. Coming to the horse's rescue, Colette tried to kick the soldiers off him, but she was pulled farther away.

Rattles stopped chasing the boy and marched to the throne to perform his favorite duty . . . smile snatching.

"Get away from me!" screamed the frightened Horseradish as Rattles approached.

The soldiers held him more firmly as Rattles reached up to the horse's mouth. Suddenly, Horseradish's whinnies stopped. Albert saw a golden glow radiating from between Rattles' metal fingers. Horseradish ceased his bucking and came to attention—frowning. He had lost his smile!

Helplessly, Albert and Colette pleaded, "No, stop it! Please give him back his smile!"

The leader rose from his throne and stepped back. He lifted the blue velvet material, exposing the locked golden chest underneath, wrapped in heavy chains. From around his neck he pulled out a long, thin chain with a large silver key attached. Bending over, he inserted the key and unlocked the massive lock which secured the heavy chains.

He cracked open the lid and a powerful glow of golden light radiated out, intermingling with the sounds of laughter.

"Hurry!" demanded No Name. "Bring that smile here. I can't stand this laughter!"

Rattles quickly moved up toward the throne with his golden bounty, but Bellvedere, still lying on the floor, lifted his right hand and circled it rapidly above his head. Using the long, severed piece of string still attached to his arm as a bullwhip, the jester lassoed Rattles' feet. The tin soldier tripped and crashed down with a clang. His hand hit the floor and Horseradish's golden smile broke free and flew high into the air.

"You fool!" shouted No Name. "Don't let that smile escape."

Rattles got to his feet and charged after the golden glow flying around the room. The other soldiers released Colette and joined in the pursuit. The glow had to keep flying higher and higher to stay out of their reach.

The soldiers climbed atop cogs and wheels, trying to get the evasive smile. Albert realized that the little glow seemed lost. It soared above the throne, and didn't know which way to fly. All of this commotion had confused it.

"Go to 'Orseradish!" he instructed, wildly pointing to the red horse.

Colette joined Albert in the yelling and pointing. "Yes, go to Horseradish."

Rattles climbed on the throne and was about to reach the smile when it suddenly recognized its owner and shot away.

"Yea," cheered Albert and Colette as the smile flew straight toward Horseradish's frowning face.

Success! The golden glow reached its target and was about to enter. But a gloved hand intercepted it. It was captured!

No Name held the glow tightly. "I suppose I have to do everything myself."

Grandly, he walked, bobbing up and down, back to his throne and pushed the frightened Rattles off the chest. Bellvedere crouched behind the box, afraid he would be reprimanded.

No Name raised the lid slightly and shoved the glow inside. Then he slammed it shut, cutting off the golden light and silencing the laughter. Horseradish's smile was his!

"There! One less toy for Christmas!"

CHAPTER TWENTY-SEVEN

The Discovery

NO NAME REPLACED THE KEY around his neck and once again his eyes met Colette's. He was troubled. Something was wrong.

Albert, standing on the music box, noticed that he had been surrounded while he had watched the chase for Horseradish's smile. The sound of sleigh bells filled the sack again. So much was at stake and time had almost run out!

"So, you are the great No Name? The one who is spoiling Christmas for so many kids?" Albert mocked.

"And you are the human boy who is trying to spoil my plans?" countered No Name. "I hate children!"

"Why do you 'ate kids so much?" Albert demanded.

"What good are they?" No Name responded. "They never play with you. They leave you on a shelf to collect dust. If they don't break you, they grow too old for you and leave you alone. What good are they?"

"Most ain't like that!" Albert defended. "If I 'ad a toy, I would take care of it and love it and when I grew up, I would give it to me own kids to play with."

No Name slammed his hand down on the Chest of Smiles. It sounded a loud bang mixed with muted laughter. He exploded, "Well, I am never going to go back into the world of children—the World of Play! I have no use for them— or you. I am going to stay right here and make sure that no toy ever leaves this place!

"No toy will ever be forced to suffer what I went through. Toys will play with toys. Let children play with children!"

"Weren't you ever played with?" questioned Albert. No Name only glared. "Well, then, you must not 'ave been a very good toy!"

"I was the best!" defended No Name. "I was the best!"

Albert challenged, "Well, what kind of toy were you?"

"None of you business!" snarled No Name.

"What was your name?" Again there was no response.

149

"Oh, I get it. You are called No Name because no one ever loved you enough to give you a name of your own. Tezzy always did say that when you love something, it should 'ave a name. Then it's special. It belongs."

"I want no more of this. Especially from a boy!" ordered No Name. "Take off his smile at once! And this time don't lose it."

Excitedly, Rattles hurried over to Albert. He had waited for this moment. The soldiers surrounded the chest to grab the boy. Immediately, they clutched his legs, pulling him down.

Albert was pushed on his back on top of the music box. There could be no escape!

"No!" screamed Colette.

Rattles marched over and reached his hand up to Albert's mouth. The boy twisted and turned trying to free himself, but the soldiers had a firm hold.

"What now?" thought the frightened boy as Rattles attempted to remove his smile.

Rattles pulled very hard causing the boy to yell out in pain. The tin soldier tried even harder—until he turned to No Name in frustration.

"It won't come off, sir."

"Pull harder!" demanded No Name.

Harder and harder Rattles pulled. "His smile can't be removed, sir," he sighed in resignation.

Albert, although still held down, began to laugh defiantly. "You can't destroy the smiles and laughter of children. Even if you do prevent Father Christmas from giving out toys, that won't stop their joy. Christmas isn't just toys! It's a feeling! A feeling of sharing and love. It's a feeling of family."

With the mention of family, Albert suddenly remembered Tezzy and his empty world. Briefly a frown erased his smile. Then he remembered the new friends he had made and felt comforted. Still, he wondered if he would ever see London again.

His thoughts were interrupted by the noise of a great commotion in the distance. The Army was returning. The sounds of screaming and pleading meant they had captured the smiling toys. Albert knew he had to act now or never.

He looked in the direction of Colette and signaled for her to break away and run. She caught the soldiers off guard and made her escape.

"Get her!" screamed No Name. "You must get her!"

"Run, Colette!" yelled the boy as he broke free from the soldiers who had been holding him. "Run!"

"I'll get her," hissed Jackaranda, who immediately spun fast in her direction.

All the remaining soldiers took on the pursuit, chasing her at full speed. Colette, out of breath, grabbed hold of the great chain leading to the cuckoo's home. She began to climb.

"Akkkk! Akkkk!" squealed the snapping bird, peeking down at the advancing Colette. "It's play time!"

Inside the hall, Albert was left alone with No Name. Suddenly he jumped from atop the jeweled music box and began to crank the handle. The haunting melody filled the ancient clock. If he was right about what he had seen earlier, his plan might work.

No Name grew agitated. The music had a tormenting hold on him.

"Stop that! Stop that at once, I tell you!" he snarled angrily.

Albert turned the handle faster and faster. The music grew louder and louder. No Name's anguish intensified.

The sounds of the approaching Army and their prisoners fused with the Master's pleas until the entire sack was filled with cries of anguish and terror. Only the music pierced the wailing.

Unprotected, No Name knew that he, alone, must stop this music in order to regain control. He leaped from his throne, bobbing up and down, and bounded toward the boy.

Albert was one step ahead. He quickly opened the mirrored lid to the music box and, careful to keep his balance, climbed up onto its narrow rim. The crank continued to turn by itself, not missing a beat.

Hastily, Albert reached down into the box and snatched a large iridescent shawl from Colette's wardrobe.

At that moment No Name tried to grab the crank handle to silence the music. But Albert swiftly tossed the netted material over the leader's head and ensnared him as he had done to that rat when cornered by Kettle and Smudge that distant day on the bank of the River Thames.

No Name panicked and struggled to free himself, but the boy deftly seized No Name's gloved hand and hauled him up to the rim of the music box.

"Let me go!" protested the captured No Name.

But his cries fell on deaf ears. Albert's attention was focused on the nearness of the advancing Army. There wasn't much time left.

"I think you like this music. I do," chided Albert to the dictator, now weakened by the haunting melody.

But the grimace on No Name's face told a different story. "Turn that off," he whined. "I . . . command you."

❋

Albert laughed and pushed the startled leader down into the storage area where Colette's clothes were kept. The many garments broke his fall. Albert leaped off and quickly shut the lid.

"I think a little privacy's what you need," teased Albert. Laughing, he climbed back on top, again put his foot on the crank, and slowly turned it. The music resonated. Faster and faster he cranked.

No Name's muffled moans could be heard from inside but Albert continued, unmoved by the pleas. No Name tried to force his way out with his remaining strength, but the boy's weight was too much.

"Stop, please!" No Name begged as the beautiful lullaby tormented him further. "Please . . . stop . . . the music!"

Then No Name's pleading gave way to sobs. Could it be? No Name crying? Was it just an act?

Faster and faster Albert cranked. The crying grew louder and louder. No Name had stopped his efforts to push open the lid. Albert jumped off the box, but continued to crank the handle. Faster and faster he went. Louder and louder the music swelled.

Shocked, Albert jumped back as the lid flew open and up popped No Name. The force of the expulsion had caused the netting and his great red cape to fall off, revealing his colorful, torn satin costume underneath.

Tears had washed most of the green paint from No Name's face, so Albert could now clearly see the real face. Incredulous, Albert recognized the brightly colored Jack-in-the-box's face.

An astonished Albert cried out, "Quigley!"

CHAPTER TWENTY-EIGHT

The Reunion

"PLEASE STOP THAT MUSIC," pleaded the tearful Quigley. "I can't bear it!"

"Quigley, it's you. I can't believe it!" shouted the amazed boy, now overcome with both joy and sadness. Albert grabbed hold of the crank and the music stopped.

"Who's . . . Quigley?" sobbed the tormented leader, confused and disoriented.

"Why, you are! You're Quigley. You were me favorite toy. I knew I knew that music. It broke me 'eart when Mr. Lacy knocked you off 'is shelf. But I couldn't stop to 'elp you," replied Albert as his mind flew to Tezzy and the events of that cold long-ago night.

"But why didn't you ever take me home to play with? Why did you leave me in the Toy Emporium?" questioned the torn Jack-in-the-box as he slowly began to recover, now that the music had stopped. "I wanted to belong, but all I can remember are those long lonely years. That beautiful melody became my cry of loneliness."

"You was too 'igh-priced for me, you was," admitted Albert. "And for everyone else in our neighbor'ood for that fact. No one could afford you because you were too special."

"But someone did want me!" thought Quigley as his mind raced back to his final night at the Toy Emporium. . . .

The old storekeeper's spirits were exceptionally jolly that last night as he climbed the ladder to dust off Quigley's shelf. A feather duster was not all that Mr. Lacy carried . . . for he brought with him a secret. "I 'ave a surprise, old music box," Mr. Lacy had chuckled. "You are to 'ave a 'ome this Christmas. A 'ome with a little boy."

The Jack-in-the-box thought his heart would burst with delight. A home! At last, after all of these years, a home!

But Quigley, packed tightly in his music box, remembered feeling a hard sudden shove. Instantly he began to tumble down and down, over and over.

Inescapably his music box crashed on the floor and splintered open, allowing him to see not only his broken self, but another shattered dream. It was then he vowed never again to seek love. And then there were the Red Wings. . . .

Quigley stepped out of his daydream and tried to suppress his tears. Slowly he was getting angrier, and soon recovered enough to work his way up from the inside chambers of the music box. He started climbing out, but he slipped and stumbled back into the box.

The approaching soldiers and prisoners were now outside the clock. Albert had to work fast.

"I 'ope this works," prayed Albert and reached into his pocket to retrieve Handyman's weapon, the golden pouch.

Quickly he opened it and like a shooting star, the golden laugh flew out. It raced around the Hall of Greatness and filled it with a warm glow.

"To Quigley," Albert yelled to the glow. "'E's inside the music box! 'Urry!"

The laughing glow stopped for only a second before it spotted its home just climbing out of the music box. The glow soared over to Quigley and flew fast circles around him. It was happy to have found him at last. Around and around it flew until it stopped in front of the clown's face. It hesitated, for it was not sure that it would be accepted. Slowly it moved closer to Quigley and gently went inside with no resistance.

Pop!

Quigley started to smile and the whole room lit up as the angry sparks crackled and flew out of his body.

"Where am I? What's going on?" the laughing Jack-in-the-box asked as the sparks faded into the air.

"I'll explain later," Albert spoke. "We've got work to do now."

The Army entered the clock and dragged the captured toys along with Handyman into the hall.

"Run, Albert!" shouted Handyman as he spotted the boy. "Save yourself!"

But Albert ran to Quigley. He had to get the silver key! Trying to remove it from around Quigley's neck, the chain got caught in one of the clown's loose buttons.

Some of the soldiers spied him. Albert yanked hard, breaking the chain, and ran with the key toward the golden chest.

Good! He was almost there!

But luck was not with Albert this time. He stumbled on the hem of the free-flowing dress he was still wearing. Quickly, he regained his stance and made it to the chest.

"Got you," surprised one of the tin soldiers as he grabbed Albert.

"Oh, no you don't," countered Bellvedere, who reached up and pushed the soldier away just long enough for the boy to put the key in the lock.

"Thanks, me friend," said the grateful Albert.

Bellvedere wanted to smile, but couldn't.

The hall was filled with soldiers and their frightened prisoners. Flip-Flop and Topp C. spotted Albert and yelled encouragement. The jacks saw their sister, Jackaranda, holding Colette, about to remove her smile, and pleaded with her to stop. Quigley, still recovering, was speechless.

"Hurry, Albert, hurry!" cried the Pretty Ones.

Success was in his grasp, when Albert felt once more the soldier's grip. Bellvedere tried to pull him off, but his strength was no match for the tin soldier. Mustering all his energy, Albert managed to keep one arm free long enough to turn the key and unlock the chest.

The heavy chains fell away and he tried to lunge forward to lift the lid.

But no! He was dragged away by the strong tin soldier. He had failed. There would be no toys for Christmas.

"I'm sorry, 'Andyman," he sobbed.

Muffled laughter emanated from the closed chest. Then the sounds of shaking and rocking caused everyone inside the hall to turn and stare. The Chest of Smiles rocked back and forth, end to end! Suddenly the lid flew open, releasing its contents.

Instantly, the room filled with a blinding golden light. The laughter of many smiles was heard. Beautiful balls of light shot high above as the smiles flew around in all directions, searching for their homes. It looked like a magnificent fireworks display.

Pop! Pop! The soldiers holding Albert were the first to be reunited with their smiles as the golden lights entered their hearts.

The frowning Horseradish had become a Grablie and charged after his once friend Albert, but was overtaken. Pop! went his smile.

"Are you all right, 'Orseradish?" inquired Albert.

Slightly dazed, the now-laughing red horse whinnied, "Why, of course. Why do you ask? What happened?"

It always took a few moments for a toy to remember what had happened once its smile was returned.

Pop! Pop! Pop! Pop!

It sounded like popcorn exploding.

The room filled with the sounds of happiness and joy. There was laughter in every corner. The ancient timepiece rocked with joy. Bellvedere cried joyful tears when—Pop! His smile found its way home.

"Where are my strings?" inquired the jester as he rose to his knees.

The toys started dancing around and around joyously. When Jackaranda was reunited with her smile the green corrosion became dust and fell to the floor to reveal her beautiful polished purple metal underneath.

But one large golden glow was having trouble. It could not find its home and was flitting from one face to another. When it reached the face of Handyman, it seemed to ask where it belonged. It was lonely.

Handyman pointed upwards. The bright golden light seemed to understand. It flew swiftly around the room and headed up towards the cuckoo's home. The toys watched and listened in fascination.

The evil black bird screeched loudly in its nest. The sounds of joy had disturbed him.

"Akkkk! Akkkk! Keep it quiet down there! Can't a birdie get some sleep?"

The glow disappeared into the top of the clock.

"Akkkk! Akkkk! Get away from me, you overlit match."

But the bird could not escape the persistent glow.

Pop!

The terrified screeching suddenly transformed into lovely warbling. "La, la, la, la, la. Joy to the world. Tweeeet, tweet, tweet, tweet, tweet. Cuckoo, cuckoo, cuckoo."

It was a time for a celebration and the toys resumed their dancing and singing.

Even the old clock, caught up in the festivities, slowly began rebuilding itself. Its great cogs and wheels started to move with precision until its rhythmic sounds tick-tocked out. The clock was now as beautiful as the day it had been built.

Fanfare began to trumpet a beautiful melody. Reunited with his smile, he was as lovely on the inside as on the outside. Even Chutney, the padded pachyderm, joined in the trumpeting to herald the celebration.

It took Rattles a few moments longer to recover totally, for his hate had been so strong. But soon he, too, joined in the play. It felt so good to laugh and smile again that the sadness and anger were all but forgotten as the happy toys celebrated their reunion.

Handyman stood to the side watching this happy scene, but finally he stepped forward and raised his ten hands.

"I hate to break this up," he shouted over the laughter and ticking of the clock, "but this *is* Christmas Eve! We haven't much time; the new toys are arriving, so everyone to his place!"

The sleigh bells rang out loudly. Thoughts of belonging and being needed by the world's sleeping children filled the air with great excitement. Off to the workshop they ran, still singing and dancing; many stopped briefly before Albert to thank him.

Handyman was watching the toys leave the hall when Quigley, bobbing up and down on his broken spring, approached with his head bowed.

"I'm sorry, Handyman, for all the trouble I've caused you."

"It could have been a disaster, all right," admitted Handyman. "You have your smile back and when you reenter the World of Play, you will find the love that you seek."

"But how do you know I'll be going back there?" he countered. "Maybe no one will want me."

Handyman smiled knowingly.

Colette walked over and placed her hand on Quigley's shoulder.

"Why?" she asked. "Why didn't you take my smile?"

Quigley, with a tear in his eye, spoke softly. "Don't you know me?"

Colette looked at him intently, but shook her head, "No, I'm sorry."

"Look closer," he pleaded.

Colette stared at him harder. Then it dawned on her. Though Quigley was torn and broken she recognized him.

Her voice broke. "We are of ze same wood. We had ze same music. Monsieur Duquesne—you were made in St. Denis by Monsieur Duquesne, ze toy maker, just as I was. I so missed you when we were parted."

"What's she talkin' about?" Albert asked as he started taking off the dress he was still wearing. "What's 'appened?"

Colette held Quigley's hand and said, "Monsieur Albert, I have ze pleasure to introduce you to my brother, ze one you call Quigley."

Albert was stunned. He knew now why he had so quickly fallen in love with the porcelain ballerina.

"Colette's my sister. We were made by the same toy maker," explained Quigley.

"Then a thief broke into the museum where we were displayed so many years ago. I was stolen and kept hidden away until one day in London. The thief's horse was spooked and crashed into a toy store. The robber's wife was so scared, she gave me to the storekeeper to keep her husband out of jail. I remained on the shelf all alone for so many years." Quigley stopped and laughed, "Why am I telling you this story, Albert? You must have heard it from Mr. Lacy a million times."

But Albert didn't mind hearing it again. It made him think of home.

"Monsieur Duquesne has given children some of the most expensive toys that the world has known," Quigley stated.

"I thought I knew your maker," Handyman mused as he put one hand gently on Quigley's shoulder. "But few others of his hand have passed this way. As you've seen, being too good, too perfect, and untouchable is not always desirable. Sometimes people are afraid to be near you."

Quigley and Colette, overcome with emotion, embraced. Their many years of separation were over—at least for awhile.

"Well, enough of this philosophizing. We have work to do. The sleeping children are waiting," scolded Handyman. "Now, work, work, work."

"Handyman," sighed Quigley. "Can you help me? I have no music box to be fitted into. I can't be a Jack-in-the-box without one. Mr. Lacy kept my music box because of the value of the jewels. It couldn't return here with me."

Colette stepped in. "Monsieur Handyman, let him have mine. You can re-fit him into it, can't you, old one?"

"Of course, I can!" exclaimed Handyman.

They all laughed. There was not much this master craftsman could not accomplish.

But Quigley stopped them, arguing, "You can't do that for me, Colette. Your music box is your life and your joy. You have taken such pride in it. You loved its music—that special music created for us. You can't give it away."

"Hush now," calmed Colette. "I've learned so much in zis great red sack. I think zat it is time I go to Ze Pond of I-Wish-I-Were to change. I should like to become a small baby doll. I could use a few more hugs than I've had these last four hundred years. I've got some more growing up to do."

"Can all that be done? Can you do it before Christmas Eve is over, 'Andy-man?" asked Albert.

"Of course. Why do you think I have so many hands?" replied Handyman, seemingly offended. "Now, let's go."

Laughing, they raced out to join the others in the loading area. But Albert stopped Handyman before they reached their destination.

"'Andyman," asked Albert happily, "can't I go to The Pond and change into a toy? I 'ave no family outside the sack to go to, even if I could get out. So if I were a toy, at least then, I could be wanted and needed."

Thoughtfully, the kindly old creature said, "Albert, my boy, that Pond is for toys only. Little boys and little girls don't need The Pond of I-Wish-I-Were to become what they most want to be. For their powers are greater. Humans carry their own 'Pond' deep inside their souls. All they have to do is believe in themselves and they can become anything their hearts dream."

Albert sighed as Handyman rushed off to greet the new arrivals and take care of any last-minute repairing.

CHAPTER TWENTY-NINE

The Good-byes

THE TOYS WAITED ANXIOUSLY at the bottom of the kaleidoscope where a bright light shone. The great red sack was being loaded. Every few seconds the kaleidoscope would open and the light would expand and become a circle. A new, never-before-played-with toy would fall through the ring, only to be welcomed and hurried to its place in line by one of the older toys. Then the kaleidoscope would close and the circle became a solitary glow once more. There was a happy commotion as the new toys were greeted and new friends were made.

Handyman hurried to the gathering to speed everyone on his way. "If Kriss Kringle had known what had happened . . . ," sighed the flustered Handyman to himself.

The nine happy jack brothers hugged their sister, Jackaranda.

"I missed you all so much," she cried. "I was afraid you would leave the great sack without me."

"No way," effused Jack-a-Dandy, "that's not our style."

"That's right, mate," added Jack-A-Roo. "We belong together."

"We would have played all our cards," countered Black Jack, "even if it meant trading our smiles to be with you."

Jackal moaned and began to shake.

Jackaranda leaned down and kissed her yellow-striped brother. "I heard you were one of the bravest in the battle outside the clock. *¿Verdad?*"

Jackal blushed bright red.

"*Ay-yi-yi,* I do love you all so much," she exclaimed.

Out of the corner of her eye she saw Dribble bouncing alone and called to him. He bounced over and she introduced him to her family.

"*Este es mi* amigo, and if it's all right with you, I would like him to join our set. No? We need a new ball because the little girl kept our old friend. What do you say, *mis hermanos*?"

Dribble was very touched by Jackaranda's offer. It would feel so good to belong once more.

"Can you bounce high?" asked Flap Jack.

Dribble started to bounce up and down and bounced way over their heads.

"He hop, hop, hops high," announced Jack Rabbit. "We should leap at the chance to snare him."

"But his color," sallied Jack-a-Dandy, "it's not regulation. A jack ball should be all red, not rainbow-colored. What would the other jack sets say?"

"I think it would make us more special," defended Jack-Of-All-Trades. "There is nothing wrong with being multicolored. I quite like it myself."

"But this mate here is hollow," challenged Jack-A-Roo. "Jack balls should be solid inside."

"I know this ball," defended Jackaranda, "and what's on the inside is not just empty air. It's special. He is filled with a loving spirit."

"I say we corral this little ball into our family," twanged Flap Jack. "What say you all?"

The jacks all agreed. Dribble had a new family.

He turned to them and cried, "S-s-shucks, s-s-something s-s-says I s-s-should s-s-say s-s-special s-s-salutations, s-s-cepting I s-s-shan't s-s-say s-s-silly s-s-sentiments, s-s-seeing I'm s-s-sure s-s-speechless."

They hugged each other as they twirled to get into line and talked of the children they would soon get to know.

The jingle bells rang out steadily now. The great journey was under way.

Colette reached The Pond of I-Wish-I-Were and took her place before its surface to gaze at her reflection. One last time she admired her beauty and elegance before she began. Over and over she repeated her chant.

"I wish I were a baby doll. I wish I were a baby doll."

Slowly, her elegant reflection faded and in its place appeared the vision of a very small, loveable baby doll. Colette dove into The Pond and grabbed her wish. When she reappeared, her transformation was complete. And although now a baby doll, she had the knowing eyes of one much older.

Colette had given up what she treasured most and had found the greatest treasure of all. Her need to be admired was replaced with a desire to give love. Her soul had learned one more lesson.

Many of the other toys were lined up, ready to be taken as soon as Kriss Kringle called for them. And every few seconds, Kriss's voice would boom and ask for a doll, train, or ball. As soon as his large hand reached into the bag, the happy toys jumped into it. Un-Bear-Able, who had become Bear-Able, already had been called to his new home.

"Goodness to gracious, I am so joyous in anticipation," exclaimed Chutney as he paced back and forth. Then it was his turn. And he was gone.

Albert ran to his friends who were waiting their turns. Topp C. was practicing his spins and low bow. Horseradish was combing his beautiful mane.

Deliah finished the repair to her dress caused by the bird's attack and was straightening out her apron as she complained, "Will you hurry up, Arabella. It's almost our turn."

"Just give me a moment more," Arabella drawled. "I'm not quite ready."

Samson strode over and asked, "Deliah, could you please flip-flop so I could say good-bye to Arabella?"

"Why, of course, honey," she smiled.

From under the red skirt, the Southern voice pleaded, "No, not yet."

But the laughing Deliah had already begun the flip-flop.

"Flop!"

Now right-side up, Arabella looked a mess. She had just put her freshly washed golden hair in pin curls to dry, using small pieces of ribbon to tie the curls. She had not expected company.

"Well . . . hello, Samson. You caught me at a bad time," the embarrassed Arabella said as she began to frantically pull the small ribbons out of her hair.

Samson leaned down and gently kissed her on the forehead. "You look lovely, peaches."

"Why, thank you, kind sir," she swooned and slightly curtsied.

"Ouch," cried Deliah, "I told you to warn me the next time you wanted to curtsy."

"Well, I just wanted to say good-bye and I hope you have a long, happy time out of the great red sack," the large iron boxer replied.

"Until next time then," she smiled.

Samson ran off to help some of the smaller toys get in line.

After he had gone, the angry Arabella lifted her skirt. "Deliah, how dare you embarrass me like that in front of my gentleman caller?"

"I thought I was being nice letting you be right-side up," laughed Deliah uncontrollably.

"Of all the nerve!" Arabella screamed.

"Flip!"

Arabella took the upside-down position to finish getting ready, leaving the black-faced Deliah on top laughing with Albert, Horseradish, and Topp C.

Colette, now a baby doll, ran to Albert. "Well, how do I look?" she questioned in her baby voice, wobbling on her untried legs.

Albert stared but didn't recognize her.

"Monsieur Albert, it is I," she said after a few moments. "I'm Colette."

"Colette," exclaimed the boy. "You look more beautiful than ever!"

Colette tried to curtsy, but fell down. Picking herself up, she tried to spin, but fell once more.

"Well, I guess my dancing days are over," she giggled, "until I take some lessons."

Albert helped her to her feet and laughed, "I think you fall down with style, I do."

Deliah, Horseradish, and Topp C. chuckled until they realized that Albert had stopped laughing.

"I'm going to miss you all," he said.

Horseradish laughed and tried to make light of the sad situation. "By noon on Christmas Day, most of us will be broken already . . . and on our way back. We'll see you really soon."

"Albert, I'm sorry you can't get out of here and go with us. I wish there was something I could do to help," Deliah sympathized.

Albert tried to hide his sorrow. "I am going to 'ave a grand time. 'Andyman said I could even be 'is assistant."

> "A spinning good time I know you'll have here,
> "And I'll get to see you maybe each year,"

remarked Topp C. confidently.

"What more could I ask for? I 'ave all the toys I ever wanted right 'ere. I'm needed 'ere. And what's more, I got no 'ome to go to out there."

Albert turned away, unable to say any more. A single tear escaped from his eye.

> "So good-bye, young Albert, my dear sweet lad.
> "For the time we shared, I am so glad,"

yelled Topp C. as Horseradish's and his time had come.

Kriss Kringle reached in for a top and a rocking horse. Instantly, they were gone.

Albert's heart ached. He slowly walked back to Handyman's shop, where Quigley was being resown and painted.

Handyman's ten arms were a blur as they moved rapidly, sewing the torn material, working on removing Quigley's broken spring, and replacing it with the spring that had almost run over Albert earlier near Colette's dingle.

"Now stay still, Boing-Boing," warned Handyman as the spring kept bouncing up and down. "I'm going to give you a new home."

"I'm, I'm, I'm, trying, trying, trying," the spring happily yelled. "But, but, but, I'm, I'm, I'm, too, too, too, excited, excited, excited."

Handyman shook his head. "What a Christmas this is! I'll be glad when it's all over. I sure hope Kriss Kringle has a lot of orders for tin soldiers this year. It'll take another century before I can get things back to normal!"

Quigley spied Albert and broke away from Handyman's loving hands.

"Come back here right now," Handyman commanded. "We don't have time for that now!"

But Quigley ignored Handyman and bounded toward Albert. He had to say good-bye to this little boy who had cared. One of Handyman's hands reached out and grabbed Quigley back.

"It's getting so you can't tell what is going to happen next around here," he muttered as he sewed the final stitches connecting the still bouncing Boing-Boing to Quigley.

Quigley, impatient to be up, sprang away as soon as the last stitch was made. He bounced to Albert.

"I owe you a lot, my friend," said Quigley. "I really could have made a mess of things."

"It's all right, Quigley," replied Albert. "You know, you really were me favorite toy. And I would 'ave taken you 'ome with me if I 'ad 'ad the money to pay Mr. Lacy."

"I know, Albert," said Quigley. "I do remember your watching me when Mr. Lacy would take me down from the shelf. And oh, how you laughed when he wound me up! I used to dream that one day I would be taken off that shelf by you for good. But I suppose as the days passed I forgot how to dream. I learned only to hate. Albert, I didn't mean what I said about children. I really do love them, but I was so lonely and it seemed like no one wanted me."

"You are going to find a little boy," insisted Albert, finding it difficult to speak. "And 'e will love you so much when you go out there this time. But remember this . . ."

Albert's speech was interrupted as tears started flowing freely from his eyes. He heard Tezzy's words coming from his own lips.

". . . There ain't nobody who's gonna love you as much as I do. Remember that!"

Albert couldn't say any more. He couldn't bear any more good-byes. Tearfully, he ran away. He didn't know where he was going; he just ran, faster and faster and deeper and deeper into The Forest.

CHAPTER THIRTY

The Shawl

IT WAS GETTING VERY LATE. As a light snow began to fall, Kriss Kringle landed his sleigh in upstate New York. He had finished depositing the gifts for all the children on this quiet tree-lined street and had to hurry if he was to beat the morning light.

Kriss settled back into his sleigh as the reindeer once again lifted him high above the snow-covered trees. But passing over one of the houses he knew to be childless, he felt he had to stop. Normally he would never break his routine, but the light in the window and the smoke billowing from the chimney seemed to call to him.

The reindeer were surprised when Kriss ordered them to land, but they obeyed and set down with ease on the new-fallen snow on the front lawn. Kriss lifted his great red sack from the back of the sleigh and went to the window to peer inside.

What he saw did not surprise him. The home was of modest means, but well appointed with comfortable furnishings. The fresh paint and lived-in quality showed this house to be occupied by loving people.

A young couple sat on the overstuffed couch staring at a blazing fire in the hearth. The low-burning candles on the large, beautifully decorated Christmas tree prominently displayed in the far corner attested to the lateness of the hour.

A perfect picture. All seemed well. But Kriss Kringle had been drawn here by a feeling—a feeling of despair. There was something missing.

He put his great sack down so he could press closer to the icy windowpane and listen in on the couple talking in low tones.

Inside, the heat from the fire held off the night chill. The husband comforted his wife, for she had been crying. He held her, soothing her.

"Seven years is a long time to grieve, my love."

"It was my fault. If only I had held on," she wept.

"You had to save that running child. You had no choice. I would hope that someone would have done the same for our son," he continued.

At the mention of "our son" the woman began to weep.

"Our son . . . I miss him so."

"He's been gone for over seven years now, Sarah. It's time for you to let go and go on," he comforted.

Sarah shuddered. Even the fire could not warm her chill.

"He's not gone, William! He's still alive, I know it!" she cried.

"That's impossible," William protested and tried to calm her. "It was a great storm. There was no way our tiny baby could have survived that large wave."

Sarah looked deep into William's eyes and said calmly and quietly, "He *is* alive. A mother feels these things."

"It's almost morning," William persisted. "Let's go to bed now. It'll be a new day when we awaken."

Sarah gently took his hand and raised it to her tear-stained face. "Just a while longer."

They embraced and held on tightly, remembering their loss. Sarah began to hum the lullaby she had used to comfort her baby Albert the day of that fateful storm. It was a strange haunting melody—one she had learned from a music box . . . as a child.

Kriss Kringle's reindeer snorted and stomped in their impatience. He realized he had lingered too long, but he glanced around the room once more, feeling compassion for this young couple on whom he had just eavesdropped. The old man's eyes wandered to the now-dwindling fire, where he noticed an empty stocking hanging on the mantel.

"Of all people on this wondrous night, I wish I had something to give you both," he said softly.

The restless reindeer urged Kriss to move on. He would have to hurry. As he strained to read the writing on the stocking, he reached down to pick up his sack. Instead of grabbing the top of the bag, Kriss's hand slipped and went inside—just as he made out the lettering on the stocking and read aloud . . . "Albert."

To Kriss's alarm, a small hand grabbed his hand from inside the sack. Confused, he pulled his hand out—with a small boy attached.

"Well, what have we here?" the jolly old man asked.

Albert was startled at the ancient's face all covered with white whiskers. He thought that after what he had just been through inside the sack, nothing could ever startle him again. Instantly, a strange feeling of calm rushed over him and he felt he was with an old friend.

"What were you doing in my sack?" questioned Kriss Kringle with a twinkle in his eye.

Albert tried to explain the best he could.

The old man laughed, "I thought I had gotten to this old sack first that night in London, but it looks like you beat me to it, young man."

"Then you must be Father Christmas, sir," the astonished boy replied.

"That I am, boy," the old man chuckled.

"I still don't know 'ow I got out. Topp C. and Horseradish said that it was impossible to leave the sack unless you were needed or wanted."

Puzzled, Kriss Kringle pondered this. His eyes gazed back into the darkened room. The fire was almost out, as his eyes rested again on the stocking. He understood.

"Your name is 'Albert,' isn't it?" he smiled warmly.

"Yes," Albert replied, "but 'ow did you know?"

Kriss Kringle turned the youth around so they both could look into the window.

"You belong here my boy. This is where you are most needed and wanted."

Confused, Albert searched the old face for an answer.

Pointing to a loving couple on the couch, Kriss said simply, "Those are your parents."

Albert was torn with emotion. He didn't know what to do. Could this be happening to him? Again he looked for answers in that knowing face.

"It's true, Albert. You belong with them."

Albert looked back into the room at these people who were his mother and father. His eyes filled with tears.

"What shall I do, sir?"

"Try knocking on the door," the bemused old man replied.

Suddenly, Albert felt the elements around him. He was cold, frightened. He remembered another night like this not so very long ago. Maybe he was only frightened by the possibility that this was just a dream, that he would wake up any moment to find himself back at the statue in the park. He had to know the truth—and started running toward the front door.

"I haven't thanked you," Kriss Kringle called out, "for saving my toys."

"What greater thanks could I want?" Albert replied and ran back to hug his new friend.

An old rooster's crow could be heard piercing the cold air of the quiet street. The reindeer made it plain that they were ready to leave.

"If there is ever anything you want, just wish hard," smiled Kriss Kringle. "If ever."

Albert stopped hugging and looked up into the gentle ancient eyes of the old man, searching.

"Quigley," he spoke softly.

"Quigley?" questioned Kriss.

"Please, sir. The Jack-in-the-box. 'E's in the sack. Can't I give 'im a 'ome, too?" Albert asked humbly.

The old man laughed and reached into his sack speaking the name "Quigley" softly. Instantly, he pulled out Colette's music box, now much smaller than it had seemed just a few minutes ago inside the sack. It was now toy size.

"Is this what you want?" inquired Kriss.

"I think so," said Albert, not really sure.

Kriss Kringle handed the music box to Albert, who immediately started to crank the handle. That strange haunting melody he had grown to love wafted through the air. But Albert was still apprehensive. Had Handyman refitted his old friend into this new home? Around and around the handle cranked, until the lid sprang open. Out popped a freshly painted, newly outfitted Quigley.

Albert and Kriss Kringle both shook with laughter at the funny clown. Was that a wink Albert saw in Quigley's eye? Or just a tear blurring his own happy eyes?

"You belong to me, me friend. I want you and need you, forever and ever. I won't ever let you get broken," promised Albert.

Albert looked up to thank Kriss Kringle, but he was gone. High above, the faint sound of jingle bells moved farther and farther away.

Clutching his little friend, Albert slowly climbed the steps to the front porch. A family!

On the door was a large brass knocker shaped like an ocean paddle-wheeler. Nervously, he reached up and touched the icy metal. Albert shuddered and quickly pulled his hand away.

A small frozen tear overflowed. "Oh, Tezzy. I am so scared. What if they don't want me? What will I do? I need you so much now."

Snow gusted around him, almost blinding him, while the wind blew right through his worn clothing. He wished Handyman had saved Tezzy's shawl. He could use it now against the chill.

Through the wind's howling and whistling, he thought he heard the voice of Tezzy calling out, "Little sailor, little sailor."

Startled, Albert quickly turned toward the sound.

The wind had whipped up the heavily falling snow. It twirled and spun around the glowing gas lamp in front of the house. The white flakes danced before the yellow light and, squinting, Albert thought he could make out the face of his beloved Tezzy, wrapped in her old shawl.

"I miss you so much, me old queen," he shuddered.

The rooster crowed his mournful cock-a-doodle-do at the coming dawn. The first rays of a new morning filtered across the horizon and the image of Tezzy slowly faded. But to Albert's amazement, the old shawl remained.

"No, this can't be real," thought the boy.

But as the sunlight grew brighter, Albert could see plainly that it was indeed a shawl. Around the dimming lamp, the old tattered yarn whirled and twirled, held up by that impertinent gust of warm wind.

Albert raced out into the front yard to the lamp. Still holding the music box, he tried to catch the spinning cloth, but it was too high.

Then the gust of wind released its treasure; with one great leap, Albert snatched it from the air.

Tezzy's shawl! It *was* Tezzy's shawl! Where had it come from? Handyman surely threw it away when he took it from Albert at the workshop—didn't he?

The boy wrapped the familiar piece of material around him. No longer could he smell the faint remnants of the carbolic soap Tezzy had always used, for Handyman must have had it cleaned. But Albert knew the memories it held could never be washed away.

Feeling the warmth of the shawl and clutching the music box tightly, Albert found new confidence. He walked back to the porch and reached his little hand up to the icy door knocker. This time, it felt warm and inviting.

"You kept your word. You said you would never leave me."

The warm gust circled once more around him to say a final good-bye. With Tezzy by his side to help guide him and Quigley in his hand to love, Albert knocked firmly on the door.

Satisfied that Albert was finally home, the warm gust blew high into the air to join its own father, the wind. Smoke billowed from nearby chimneys as rested hearths were relit and the smell of breakfast filled the air. The sun shone brightly now; for Tezzy had been right . . . it was indeed a new day.

THE BEGINNING